Mrs. Eugenia J. Bacon

Lyddy

A tale of the old South

Mrs. Eugenia J. Bacon

Lyddy
A tale of the old South

ISBN/EAN: 9783337000394

Printed in Europe, USA, Canada, Australia, Japan

Cover: Foto ©Andreas Hilbeck / pixelio.de

More available books at **www.hansebooks.com**

LYDDY

LYDDY

A Tale of the Old South

By

EUGENIA J. BACON

MDCCCXCVIII
CONTINENTAL PUBLISHING CO.
25 PARK PLACE, NEW YORK

CONTENTS.

7

PREFACE.

OFFICERS and men that for four years struggled to tear down the Stars and Stripes, are to-day proudly planting Old Glory over a land oppressed by cruelty. In the words of Commodore Dewey, "There is no South, no North, but one united country."

Old lines of differences are for ever obliterated.

Descendants of Lee and Grant shouldered arms, and have been standing side by side, doing battle, at the will of the American Government.

And in this cause of humanity men that were once bound by the yoke of servitude are taking an active part.

Southern negroes have now enjoyed the blessings of freedom for more than thirty years, yet their faithfulness and devotion remain fresh in the minds of former owners; even as the harrowing scenes depicted by Mrs. Harriet Beecher Stowe continue to attract throngs of men, women, and children to theatres and halls.

Those of the race that were born slaves will soon have passed away, therefore I deem it a fit

time to flash the sunshine of Lydia's life before
the eyes of the rising generation; so that they
may realise that, in face of the cruelties depicted
in "Uncle Tom's Cabin," there were, on the other
hand, many such characters as Lydia, with black
skins but pure souls.

My resolution to write Lydia's history came
unexpectedly to me while visiting in Edinburgh,
Scotland.   One evening, at dinner, our party
were discussing national dishes, when my vis-a-
vis inquired of me what, with us, corresponded
to their haggis.

" Hog and hominy," I answered.

"Then you must be a Southerner!" she exclaimed.

"Yes, an old-fashioned slave-owner; happily
reconstructed, however, so as not only to rejoice,
but be harmless."

My friend's little girl, sitting near, looked up
with a startled expression.   Oblivious to her
surroundings, she laid aside her knife and fork,
pushed her chair from the table, and hastened to
her mother's side.   "Was she really a horrid
slave-owner?" she faltered.   Then her tears fell
freely.

Only a few days before, she had, for the first
time, it appeared, witnessed the theatrical repre-
sentation of "Uncle Tom's Cabin."

But the pathetic words of this innocent child
awakened me: she little knew that the very in-
stitution by which my life was once surrounded,
had been established first in America by her own
English-speaking ancestors. I determined there
and then to write Lydia's life as I knew it.

So, dipping my pen into the inkstand of
Slavery days, homely scenes of joy and sadness
are narrated as they really happened in the life of
one of God's black angels, whose wings were
stained by sin.

E. J. B.

LYDDY:

A TALE OF THE OLD SOUTH.

I.

Sold at Auction.

" While wild in wood the noble savage ran."

LYDIA'S grandparents had danced in their primitive state on Africa's sunny shore. She, however, was born a slave, yet her faith and·trust in God was pure and abiding, ensuring to her the love and devotion of all about her.

In stature she was of medium height, her skin a glossy black, with broad forehead and great, loving, tender eyes. Unlike most negroes, too, her nose was not very flat, nor her lips thick, and, in laughing, she showed a double row of faultless teeth.

Her apparel was always simple,—a white apron and a coloured turban being the most conspicuous

13

parts of it. In her back hair was stuck a large
plain tortoise-shell comb—a gift from her mistress,
whose grandmother had worn it when such ornaments were stuck high in the coiffure.

No Turk coils his soft white muslin more grace-
fully than Lydia coiled her bright bandanna.
And with the shell to uphold its folds, there was
a certain individuality in its symmetrical arrange-
ment. Other negroes might don hats and furbelows on Sunday, but Lydia, No. Over a half-
worn dress of her mistress, she tied her own spotless tucked apron, gave a twist to her bandanna,
—and she was dressed in her best.

Proud of her position in the nursery, she digni-
fied it with rare good sense, and thus endeared
herself not only to the children, but also to all
our visitors.

Lydia was born on the estate of one Samuel
Jameston, an Englishman, living near the village
of Riseburg. Her father Belfast held the position
of foreman on the place, and her mother Nancy
that of cook. And what a cook!—sending to the
squire's table the richest gumbo, the lightest and
hottest waffles, and the fluffiest of biscuits.

When but a girl Lydia's master died, leaving
an only child, Samuel, already motherless, in
possession of Fairfield. And so, in time, the old
homestead, with its massive English sideboard

supplied with the choicest of wines and finest of cigars, became, with the young master at the head, a rendezvous for fast young men, fond of hunting and driving. The metaphorical latch-string hung outside the door, as it ever hangs in many Southern houses, and invited friends to enter. But nights of revelry for the men were followed by mornings that were trying to the heart of old Nancy.

"If Mars Sam don't git him a wife what will keep him sober, Nancy must quit de kitchin!" she often cried in bitterness.

One person alone on the plantation had any power over Samuel when he was not himself; and that was old Chloe, who had nursed him from infancy. With her black face wreathed in smiles, —notwithstanding the tears of distress welling up at the sight of "her boy's" red eyes,—she often soothed him as none other dared to do. One morning, quite accidentally, Nancy detected Chloe's occult power, when she heard her outside the library door, praying:

"O blessed Lord! I is done all I kin fer Mars Sam; certain an' sure de big Devil is laid hold o' my boy. O Master, you what 'buked de storm a ragin' on de sea, come down wid dy mighty power an' say, 'Git behin' me, Satin.' Sure, my w'ite chile will 'spect de, O Lord. At chu'ch

Mars C. C. tells us if we prays an' believes, dat de Lord will answer. He will, only we must wait, 'umble-like. Oh, God! ole **Chloe** is a-waitin'!"

Nancy's cares increased : her husband sickened, and died. Then a less experienced man was made foreman at Fairfield.

After this the crops in a measure failed, debts were increased, until, at last, it became necessary for the young master to sell his negroes, one after another.

Lydia accordingly was advertised to be "knocked down" to the highest bidder, at Riseburg, January 20, 1830. Her mother—determined to seek for her a good master—came and implored my father—living at a small place called Navarre—to buy her.

" Massa, she's as likely a gal as you kin find, an' will make a smart housemaid fer de young lady folks says you's goin' ter bring ter Navarre."

Riseburg, it may be added, was the county-seat, and boasted of a court-house, two stores, one tavern, and a half-dozen residences.

At the stores negroes exchanged eggs and chickens—not always their own, alas !—for sugar, calico, and tobacco.

A dilapidated stage-coach, which ran between Savernake and Darius, stopped at the tavern.

Here passengers refreshed themselves on "hog and hominy," accompanied, whenever wanted, with sweet yams and corn-bread.

Moreover, on certain days in the year, a shrewd business man, with a twang in his voice not Southern, mounted a block or a live-oak stump in front of the court-house, and, in auction style, "knocked down" to the highest bidder negro after negro.

In this wise Lydia fell to my father; and, after a touching farewell with her mother, she was driven away, seated beside the coachman Marlborough.

Before parting, however, Nancy gave her good advice, and likewise overwhelmed Lydia's new owner with thanks:

"De Lord bless you, massa, an' help my gal ter sarve you well, so you won't neber be sorry of your barg'in."

Not long after, Lydia waited at the front steps for her master's bride, whom she conducted to her chamber. Before adjusting her mistress's slippers, she kissed the tiny feet in token of welcome, and said, "We is all on us goin' ter love you lots, missy." A dainty hand patted her gay bandanna in appreciation of love so fervently shown; for, in slavery days no stiffness existed between mistress and maid.

2

Nancy frequently spent Sundays at Navarre, and when her son Belfast was sold, he joined his sister, to the delight of their mother, who was bravely doing her duty, separated as she was from her only children.

" It's not fer long dat I must work 'lone," she groaned, "caise dey'll soon lay me 'side de ole man, an' from my grave a song 'll rise, caise we two chilluns is in de hands of a Godfearin' good master."

Her prophecy—at least as to her daughter's ability—proved correct. For, when the position of nurse was to be filled, Lydia was given charge of the child.

Navarre was sold eventually, and a large and beautiful estate, comprising three thousand acres, known as Green Forest, was purchased. Its homestead, or dwelling, was of little importance ; but its rambling old roofs and overhanging ledges were embowered in a forest of eternal green. In February the yellow jessamine, trailing from tree to tree, gave the grove a wealth of golden beauty, and in spring the magnolia, king of flowers, scented the air with its large bowl-like blossoms. Interspersing these, festoons of long grey moss floated in the summer breeze, or whirled in winter's wild blasts from live-oak, pine, and olive trees.

To describe the singular effect produced by this curious growth of the Far South, is impossible. Swaying from innumerable tree-limbs, its smoky colour and its spectral shapes impart a gloom even in the midst of spring's gayest tints, or mid-summer's blaze of full-blown flowers. Were it possible, indeed, to exterminate this growth, which is not a parasite, the human race could not exist in the miasmatic air that gives it nourishment.

The house at Green Forest needing to be enlarged and renovated, a mason was given the contract. A skilled workman from Savernake, he was also a free negro; and so he inspired the plantation people with due respect. For, at that period, few men with coloured skins were their own masters.

It was not long, however, before Marlborough, the coachman, manifested an intense dislike for the newcomer.

"I's what folks calls a slave, but I wouldn't change place wid dat copper-coloured fellow. He's his own boss, but from sun up ter sun up he must work ter earn his hog an' hom'ny.

"Massa's folks sits outside deir cabin, pickin' de banjo, de sun high ober head : Caise why? dey has finished deir day's task. As fer horses, show me a man what reins a finer pair in Siberty

county dan Bolivar an' Bonepart, an' in no carriage sets a liklier nurse dan we Lyddy. Any
coachman would be proud ter drive her round."

But in spite of these self-gratulations and this
show of contentment, a suspicion was rankling in
his mind that the free negro might some day come
between him and the woman he loved. In fact,
he had already noted signs that indicated that the
tender eyes of the nurse had captivated the heart
of the mason.

He longed to know how matters were progress-
ing; so he secreted himself behind a low-limbed
myrtle bush near where Lydia usually sat when
"her babies" were snugly tucked away in bed.
Yes, there they were now!—he heard Marmaduke
pleading:

"My lady, I loves you wid all my heart. Say
you'll be mine, an' I'll pay down gold an' silver
fer you, an' present you wid your own self.
You'll be a free lady then, wearin' fine silk frocks
an' a hat wid long plumes like de w'ite folks.
Jes be mine an' I'll give you a gal ter wait on you.
I knows well dat coachman is in love wid you, but
he's got nothin' ter offer you ; he's a slave tied ter
his master's whippin' post. I'm a free man!"

"Massa sets a pow'ful stoh by we coachman ;
he ain't tied ter no post. We's growed up ter-
gether ; so I knows."

A shout of delight was but scarcely suppressed from behind the myrtle bush.

" But, my lady, wouldn't you like ter be mistress of your own house ? If you'll be mine, I'll buy you a home soon as I gits paid fer de work here. I knows what it is ter be a slave. When my master, who was also my father, died, he left me free. T'ank God, my han's is got no chains on dem now. I does as I please."

" But you must work fer your victuals an' clothes! So Bro' Molbro was sayin' in de kitchin."

" He's a fool, dat man. Don't you listen ter his talk. I'm my own boss an' does jes as I likes. You be mine, an' you kin do de same."

Marlborough's heart thumped as if made of lead. The realisation of his inability to compete with one able to buy his own wife, giving her, too, a house and housemaid, completely over- whelmed him. Hitherto, the wish for heaps of gold had never marred his happy life ; but now, —how could he earn enough to overbid his hated rival was his dominant thought. Convinced, finally, that his only chance lay in persuading his master not to sell the nurse, and also to dismiss the mason, getting some one else to complete the work, he determined, if these failed, to way-

lay Marmaduke and batter his yellow face into
jelly. Lydia then wouldn't care to marry him.

With a woman's discerning eye, the mistress
divined that there was trouble existing, and that
the wedding-feast she had hoped to order for
two of her house-servants would not be for the
coming Christmas.

My father promised Marlborough not to part
with the nurse; but he could not annul the contract with Marmaduke, except for incapacity.
Marmaduke, however, as has been said, was a
skilled workman.

"Oh, massa! I never gits a word wid we
nurse dese days. If I does ketch up wid her,
she talks 'bout elegant gentlemens what does as
dey please. Massa, can't you hire Mr. Jackson
ter finish de work?"

He was told No!

But his longed-for chance to speak to Lydia
soon came. He had been sent to the grove to
summon the nurse home. There he found her
seated on a log, her white children gathering wild
violets. Forgetting his mission, he gave vent to
his feelings.

"Lyddy, dey is no time fer coteship, you
knows you is de idol of my life; you knows I'd
die fer you. But, Lyddy, I has no money ter
buy you; I has no house but what massa'll build;

I can't give you a gal ter wait on you, but, my love, I'll wait on you myse'f ; I'll be ter you all dat any black man kin be ter a lady. Tell me, Lyddy, tell me, is you goin' ter marry dat hateful vagabon' of a yaller niggar?"

Lydia, startled and stunned to find he had gained information of her private affairs, merely tossed her head and said : " Bro' Molbro, is you lef' your work' jes ter come here ter tarrify me? What concern is it o' yourn' if I do choose ter be de mason's wife? You go an' tend ter your own business."

" Lyddy," he said, " W'en I shets my eyes at night, dat great merlatter man stands over me bellowin' ' Hands off ! ' I ain't fer makin' a racket on Green Forest, but some night I's goin' ter hit dat fellow plumb ter kingdom come."

As if the deed were already done, Lydia burst into tears. " Will you be a murderer, like Cain !— Oh ! Oh !"

Her white children gathered at her side and covered her with caresses. " Mommer, don't cry ; who has hurt you?"

Marlborough one day confided his troubles to his master. Consequently, a letter was written to Savernake, making inquiries as to Marmaduke's marital relation,—suspicion, in fact, having whispered that he was already married. Letters at that date were carried on horseback, the post-age costing twenty-five cents.

An answer came, in due time. The mason *was* a married man, with three children, his home on the outskirts of Savernake.

This news brought joy to the coachman, and his face beamed with delight. Now it would be plain sailing,—his pathway clear. For no man, even " a free niggar," could marry two wives.

The songs in the nursery, once gay and bright, changed into funereal dirges, while the negroes at the quarters, lustily abused " de no 'count free niggar who had fooled de whole plantation, specially de likliest 'oman of de crowd."

Marmaduke, now in disrepute, hired an assist-ant, finished his work, and returned to Savernake, caring nothing about the misery he left behind.

II.

Preacher Frank's Prayer.

"In the mud and scum of things
Something always, always sings."

YEAR by year Green Forest was enlarged and beautified, its many buildings so arranged as to give the plantation the appearance of a village.

A wide avenue opened from the Savernake and Darius turnpike. Large overhanging trees entwined on either side, their limbs forming an arch festooned with grey moss, rays of sunlight here and there darting through to the sandy way. One could get merely a glimpse of the Colonial homestead, with its cream-coloured Corinthian columns.

At right angles with the avenue, a street led to the Sandyrun Road. Its length was dotted with buildings, and row after row of negro houses, a small enclosure in the rear of each for a vegetable-garden. The cabins were not made of logs, but of deal, with brick chimneys.

Midway of this street was a circular enclosure, its lattice-paling hidden by a wealth of Cherokee roses, their glossy green leaves and creamy flowers glistening in the noonday rays. And here hung an up-swinging pole, with its moss-covered bucket. Little moss, however, collected, so constantly was the bucket on the dip, its sparkling contents quenching the thirst of hundreds in the quarters.

A few yards to the left glistened a small duck pond,—the rendezvous for geese and ducklings. Splashing and cackling in delight, they were surrounded often by troops of black piccaninnies, squeezing soft mud between their toes.

Surmounted by a crowing cock, symbolic of poor Peter's treachery, stood a church with a pointed tower; in the rear a grave-yard hedged round with young cedar trees.

Nothing in modern machinery could be more wonderful and impressive to us than was our cotton-gin. The building simulated a summer-hotel, with a wide uncovered piazza, for drying raw-cotton—the principal staple of the place. Day after day Uncle Toby sat in front of a keyboard with sharp savage-looking teeth, running handsful of cotton to and fro, from base to treble. But no musical sound came, save the rattling of jet-black seeds into a hamper below as the liberated fleece, like flakes of snow, whirled into a windowless room. This we longed to enter, but our foreman, Scipio, never allowed us within five feet of the threshold.

"Is you chilluns a-wantin' ter be suffocated? Sure's you puts your nose inside dat dooe, you is done fer, jes as good as if you is buried six foot underground."

We were sure a few moments in that fairy chamber could do no harm. But the foreman was wise. From openings in the gin-house floor long bags were suspended. Down into these, negro men, with heavy pestles, compressed five hundred pounds of cotton. Modern invention— the great compress—does this work in a few minutes.

Near the sea, on our rich bottom lands, the cotton plant attained a growth of fully six feet, its branches covered with pale yellow blooms with purple centres. These crinkle into an elongated pod, resembling a hickory-nut ; and when brown and dry pop into four quarters, from which a wealth of fleece quivers in the slightest breath of air. On clear autumnal days, the tall sepia-coloured stalks appeared dry and lifeless ; yet, day after day, soft snow-white tufts hung from myriad branches, thus outlining a picture long to be remembered.

Near the pond, grouped picturesquely, were

other buildings : the saw-mill, with its piles of logs seasoning in the sun ; and a circular wheel, where three horses tread, advancing not an inch.

A ride on this revolving circle was our delight. And Daddy Joe had frequently to rescue us from perilous positions.

After a Jewish synagogue the blacksmith shop was designed ; and opposite to it was an imposing structure, replete with rice threshers, circular saws, and turning-lathes. Home-grown maple or oak was fashioned there into furniture ; for, negroes that married on the place were "set up" in housekeeping.

Against the chimney corner of his cabin young Bill often leaned his bench, tingling a besmeared banjo. Sweltering over an open fire, Dinah, his bride, fried slices of bacon, while the corn loaf browned in a ring-top oven.

"De pone am' done. Come, Bill, les' eat supper."

From tin plates they ate their rations ; serving them out, too, in no meagre quantity.

Dancing in the brick-yard always followed the lighting of kilns. Lydia took "her children" as lookers on ; she herself dared not hook arms in the giddy whirl ; Parson C. C. was far too strict to countenance such frivolity in his church members.

Christmas festivities held a prominent place in the minds of both workers and children. Before the Pleiades faded into the light of morning, we were astir, eager to say first " Merry Christmas ! "

" Now deir is dat blessed chile done kotch me ! Here, honey, is a fresh aigg jes dropped yisterday."

We disbursed our debts from a hamper of cakes.

A bell summoning us to breakfast, stalwart negro men would perch us upon their shoulders, —our arms clasped about their woolly heads. So they trotted home, at a pace dangerous to life and limb. An army of little blacks in our rear whooped and screamed with delight. Many of them, in fact, in hot haste to join the fun, forgot to complete their morning toilet, appearing without certain essential garments.

No queen ever enjoyed a triumphal procession, with its pomp and show, more than we did our home-going on Christmas morning. Our doll tables were for a time replete with eggs,—boiled, fried, whisked, or scrambled, with nuts for dessert.

Southern children lived among such environments, petted and spoiled by faithful slaves.

In front of the church, on Christmas evening

bright bonfires burned, illuminating a table burdened with barbecued meats, potatoes, bread, and
cakes for the plantation feast. Negro women
wore their gorgeous head-turbans and gayest
dresses, furbelowed and flounced to the waist-
line, while the men donned their whitest shirt-
fronts and brightest neckties.

Upon the arrival of the white family, the signal
to begin was given. Scipio, the master of cere-
monies, usually asked his master for a blessing.

Daddy Frank lifted both hands reverentially,
after my father's voice ceased : "De Lord help we
niggars ter be true an' faithful ter we w'ite folks
what has spread dis here bounty fer we spacious
'joyment."

The foreman then added, with commanding
tones, " Hunno people, stand at a 'spectful distance
till de w'ite folks is sarved, den you may set to
but be sure you eats dis luscious meal in a decent
an' proper manner."

Dancing followed the refreshments, interspersed
with the cutting of an imaginary "pigeon's wing."
This, as may well be inferred, requires an agile
body.

The noise and frolicking that followed were not
produced by stimulants ; it was but the unchecked
outburst of happy hearts. Though the negroes
possessed no money, they, in reality, had an un-

failing savings bank to draw upon whenever ill-health or old age overtook them; in short, they felt that they had a right to care and protection, and so holiday amusements served as cords to bind even tighter the owned and the owner.

Merry-making was not confined to the quarters alone, for the homestead itself was rarely ever free of guests. This, of course, entailed extra domestic work, yet the servants gloried in a house full of people.

Even now, as many gentlemen know, negro men, are experts in clothes-brushing. It would also be difficult to find a better maid than a negro girl accustomed to attend on her mistress. So, when it became necessary to dismiss Lydia from the nursery, mother's cares were greatly increased, and Phœbe, who succeeded her, had a hard time:

"Go 'way! you sha'n't dress us; we want mommer to button our clothes. Leave go our curls, you're a horrid black niggar, we want mommer with her red bandanna and white apron. Why don't mommer come in the mornings; why has she left us to rake up old leaves?" This fighting and howling went on in the nursery until it almost distracted our mother.

Letha said one morning, "Phœbe, you sha'n't talk about mommer, she's not bad, she is the best

mommer in the world. Her skin *is* black, but
God can make it white as snow. Some day she'll
be a pure white angel and we'll walk with her in
Paradise, she told us so herself before she left."

And though Lydia had been overwhelmingly
humbled, our first thought in the morning
was always to run in the direction of the
" trash gang,"—as the convalescent workers were
termed.

Lydia, at sight of her " w'ite chilluns," dashed
her rake to the ground and clasped one after another to her bosom, covering their chubby hands
with kisses.

" Do, chilluns, beg missus ter let me come
home ! I wish I was daid ; how can I lib away
from my pets? Is I neber goin' ter be forgiven ? "

Her hot tears were quickly brushed away by
baby fingers.

She was not the only one on the plantation
that was utterly miserable. Marlborough was
simply desperate. Not because he was a slave ;
not because his pockets were empty of gold and
silver. It was because there seemed no prospect
of his marrying the woman he loved. Indeed, if
she but caught sight of him she either hastened
away or hid her face. Gossip accordingly grew
rife among the field-hands, many assuring Marlborough that he wasted his life waiting for a smile

from a woman that vowed she had no confidence in any man, and wouldn't marry the best unless he could give her a house and housemaid, with purchase papers in her own name, making her thus a free woman.

With no opportunity to ask her if it be true, the last vestige of hope was crushed, and, man-like, Marlborough sought to comfort himself in the company of another woman. His amatory attention was given to a field-worker younger than Lydia, who lived on Mr. Joe Lamont's plantation, —three miles distant. Their courtship was brief; scarcely three weeks.

He gave Flora, the night he married her, a plain gold ring with marks inside,—unintelligible to her untutored mind.

A ginger-coloured baby arrived in course of time in Lydia's cabin. And when we were permitted to visit them, she again and again entreated to be taken back. " Beg missus ter forgive me, an' let me come home."

Early in summer, wearing a spotless apron and crimson head handkerchief, she resumed her former position, greeted with a clapping of tiny white hands and screams of joy.

In a year's time she gave the lie to gossip, and was married at Pleasant Grove church by Dr. C. C. to James, servant of Colonel Cummings.

3

James gathered oysters and fish for his master; and he kept " us " well supplied with lovely sea-shells; our toys, in fact, were the handiwork of different coloured men on the estate.

Lydia's hands and life were full, caring for a number of children, who embraced every opportunity to mount bareback horses, climb trees, get over " stake and rider fences," acting, in fact, like lambs in pasture—never still a minute. In our pranks the negro workers helped us, incurring censure rather than report our misdeeds. I recall one dreadful experience:

Beside the saw-mill stood long box-like structures, designed to flood or keep dry rice-fields Sawney had started with four easy-going oxen, carrying one box suspended between lumber wheels. Letha, always my leader, suggested the fun of exploring the other.

"You go in yonder end!" said she, " we will cross in the centre." We did not think of dimensions.

As an infant endeavours to get at its playthings scattered on the nursery floor, so we essayed to go through the rice-field trunk. Our creeping for a time was seemingly unimpeded, then nails protruded, rending pinafores, dresses, pantalets and stockings, not to mention delicate skin.

We both, in short, possessed a goodly store of

perseverance—for wrong-doing; on the principle, probably, that stolen fruits are sweet.

We eventually reached the centre of that low, narrow thirty-foot box; but to pass each other was quite another feat.

If a cat's head goes through an opening, the body easily slips in. We two might have kissed, but there we stuck, nails above, nails below, splinters on every side pinning us fast in our perilous position. Our tears intensified the darkness.

" Ding-dong, ding-dong," sounded the dinner-bell, stimulating our healthy appetites.

Lydia called, " Letha, Dodo, way is you? De dinner bell is gone. Come quick, aunt Affie is got a big sweet pudden fer you ! "

Leading his horses to the pond to drink, Marlborough stopped for a tête-à-tête with Lydia.

" Bro' Molbro, is you seen my chilluns, dat only a minute ago was makin' a block-house? Here is deir bonnets, but where's dem two tomboys ? "

Though now a married man, Marlborough's heart still burned with the old love ; so, wishing her to tarry, he replied, " The children will come soon."

" No ; I hears dem cryin' ; Dey must be up some tree."

He tied his horses to a branch, and together

they examined low-limbed trees, where, before, we had been found pinioned to thorns, our aprons in shreds.

The thud of horses' hoofs jarred us and we heard our nurse's voice still calling.

" Mommer," we screamed, " here we are ! Take us out, we can't move an inch."

" Honey, way is you? De pudden is gittin' cole. Law, bless my soul, Bro' Molbro, if here ain't my two chilluns in de rice-field trunk."

Marlborough grasped the situation, and, with deafening blows of an axe, liberated us. He then gently lifted us to our feet, a mass of shreds—blood-stained—hanging about our scratched arms and legs.

Lydia hastened home and dressed us for dinner, her face wearing an innocent expression. We wouldn't be punished if she could prevent it ! Our clean frocks mother noted ; and this, with her sympathizing words as to bruises on our hands, cut into our guilty hearts.

"I don't want any pudding to-day, do you, Dodo ?" Letha whispered. " Mother, will you excuse Dodo and me ? There are cardinal birds picking about our trap ; perhaps one is caught."

She was closing the dining-room door when a gentle voice said, " I would like to speak to my little girls in the nursery before they go out."

Alas ! Our pudding was uneaten, and we were entrapped, instead of red birds.

Quick as a flash Lydia quitted her post beside the infant's high chair ; for she did not wish the débris on the nursery floor to shock her mistress.

Of course punishment ensued ; for we might have been suffocated but for timely aid. Besides, we had often been warned not to put even our noses inside the water-gates.

" Which would you mind most, Letha, going to bed or having a switching, " mother asked.

" Switch me and let me go to my trap," she replied, crying as if her heart would break.

" And you, Dodo ? "

" Let me go to bed, please ; I'm so tired, I don't want to play any more to-day."

She took me by the hand, and calmly turned to Lydia :

" Put Letha to bed. "

" Oh, missus, you is made a mistake ; it's Letha don't min' switchin'. "

Waving her into silence, mother gave us that which was most disagreeable. And while I made the welkin ring, Letha lay robed in white, snugly tucked in bed.

Rightfully, I should have been one of the best of children,—if prayers of the righteous avail.

In turning leaves yellow with age, I once read a prayer earnestly offered in my behalf that my father had transcribed.

On all well-regulated plantations it was a custom to record daily events. Accordingly, from my father's diary I now quote a few paragraphs, which may give an insight into the relationship existing between master and slave :

GREEN FOREST, *Feb. 2d*, 18—.

The sun rose clear this morning, blending its rosy light with a profusion of full-blown peach blossoms. I stood at the nursery window, after an anxious night, watching my field-hands going to work, shouting and rejoicing over the birth of another little girl-mistress. God grant that the wee infant, cradled in its mother's arms, may be a comfort in days to come to my negroes. In God's love may she and her slaves ever rest.

February 9th.

According to old-time negro custom, many brought offerings of chickens and eggs for the new-born child, entreating that they might have one peep at its face. "Mother" feared the exposure, but I could not resist their entreaties; one by one they peered into the soft folds of flannel for a wee baby face nestling in Lydia's arms.

Lydia's proud look showed she hoped that the child, Saccharissa Alice, would reign some day a princess of royal blood.

The name, too, delighted the old women. "Sure," said they, " it's high time missus had a namesake."

In truth, this name had been given to two other daughters, each in turn, however, christened otherwise. One of Lydia's favorite rhymes seems quite apropos.

She represents cocks welcoming in the dawn. One crows lustily : "Woman rules here." Answered : "So she does here." An overgrown Shanghai seeming to say, " And everywhere."

SUNDAY, *Feb.* 14*th.*

Frank, our coloured preacher, is not an ordained minister, but has been set apart by our pastor and elders at Midway church as a watchman over Green Forest. He has authority to perform the marriage-rite, but not to administer the sacrament. He preaches in the negro chapel, every Sunday night where prayer-meetings are held during the week. I attend, by way of encouragement. To-night he opened the meeting with an earnest appeal to the Lord in behalf of the "dear good missus an' her baby."

"O blessed Master, keep dy best benediction fer de young child what is come to us 'long wid de early dew an' de mornin' star. We is hear read 'bout a star what shine ober Israel, when de brederen was a-callin' from de watch tower, 'What of de night?' No answer come, only one little star a-twinklin' an' a-twinklin' till lik' a cloud of fire it rise an' stopped ober de manger where de blessed Lord was a-layin'. It ware a joyous break o' day, when de sheperds found deir Saviour a-sleepin' 'long side beasts o' de field. Dey straightway took de best of all dey had an' laid it at de feet of de young child. An angel of love

is give us a new missy, an' we none on us kin know what
a blessin' dis blessed baby may be to us when we is old
an' feeble. Lord, do hold dy holy hand before de baby's
face so de debil can't so much as peep at um."

Frank then took the text, " Unto us a child is born."

His scripture quotations are ludicrously twisted, his
reasoning powers abstruse, but beneath his tortuous
paraphrases is a deep sense of God's love and his own
unworthiness."

March 13*th.*

To-day, at Midway, the baby was christened Eugenia
Amanda ; but she is nicknamed Dodo.

III.

Eaten by a Bear.

" Do lovely things, not dream them all day long ;
And so make life, death, and that vast forever
One grand, sweet song."
CHARLES KINGSLEY.

EARLY in the seventeenth century Midway church was erected by English settlers. General Stewart of Revolutionary fame used it as temporary quarters for his cavalry-men, their horses tramping over or lying beside graves of men who gave their lives for the mother-country.

Wealthy planters of Siberty County worshipped here, descended, as they were, from old Puritan stock who pinned their faith on Westminster Catechetical doctrines. For many years its pulpit was occupied by the Rev. Abel Holmes, whose son, the illustrious poet Oliver Wendel Holmes, retained ever a sympathy with and tenderness for the Southerner.

At this period every one went to church, even

babies of a few months' old, plantations being virtually deserted on the Lord's day.

The choir sat in the centre of the church gallery, and was led by one playing a flute. The negroes, many of whom were members in good standing, occupied the two sides.

The first Sunday in each quarter the Lord's table was spread in front, just below the high oaken-carved pulpit. After the whites were served with bread and wine, their slaves descended, taking the vacated chairs. To their thick lips they lifted reverentially a silver chalice. No one—sinner or backsliding Christian—ever left before the celebration. And—as with me—these long communion-table pictures are, I know, indelibly impressed upon the minds of many that are now hoary-headed. Indeed, well do I recall the high-backed pews, at the head of which sat a man, but never a woman. For, years before, men were armed with flint and steel guns, which they stood in the corner of the pew, ready for use.

Indians, in those days lurked about, springing unexpectedly upon these pious folk. So, while the gentlemen listened to the voice of the preacher, who expounded for one hour the doctrines of predestination and kindred subjects, they were also on the alert for the approach of the red man. In the tents or in the two-room shanties surrounding the church, lunch was served. Our cook Affie prided herself on the quality of her cold turkey and ham, accompanied with rice loaf and other delicacies.

Friends interchanged visits before afternoon-service, while the old folks strolled among the graves in the cemetery, reflecting, doubtless, how near the bottom of life's hill they were.

With no thought that fresh sod would some day be upturned to receive them, young people sat on the moss-grown tombstones, flirting or laying bright plans for future lives of love.

After these long services at Midway, we were allowed to roam about the Green Forest Grove, stopping at the pond to note how young ducklings spent their seventh day. Here, too, we found black boys and girls dabbling in soft sticky mud, though their mothers, before going to church, had scrubbed and dressed them for the week.

" See missy red frock ! Jes, look at he tippet ! "

" Dat's my missy what's got yaller spots an' a w'ite aprin wid wheels 'round de bottom."

" It's no sech t'ing ; dat's Juno missy; ma done say so."

" You is a liar ! Dat's Juno missy wid de gold shoes (bronze) an' w'ite stockens."

" Oh, you is a big liar ! "

" Stop, children," I remonstrated. " You shouldn't call each other liars. Did you never hear of Ananias and Sapphira who told lies and God struck them dead."

" No, ma'am ; no ma'am. Tell we 'bout Anas an' Saphe."

On this wise, truths taught us were repeated to groups of eager piccaninnies : how Samuel was called and replied, " Here, Lord, am I "; how Joseph's coat of many colours was found. Thereafter Sunday stories became a Sabbath amusement. It rained one afternoon, and Lydia gained permission for us to meet in the wash-house, thus beginning a Sunday-school that continued for years.

With the children came a thick-set old woman to be taught. She wore a three-cornered rag tied across her head ; her hair, streaked with grey, and with stray blanket threads as well, was never molested by curry-brush or comb. Aunt Sallie had neither kith nor kin. She expended her best efforts to keep other persons' offspring quiet on week days ; and on Sunday, not caring, it seems, to avail herself of this one chance of rest, she came to Sunday-school.

For convenience, and to prevent being ejected from a place, she brought under her arm a plank, at each corner of which was a securely-plugged upright strip. Plumping this bench beside the fireplace, she settled herself against the chimney jamb, her legs stretched, one heel dug into the ash-covered hearth, its mate placed on top, while her ten toes moved restlessly, resisting the effect of a scorching oak-fire. When Samuel's name was called, she enthusiastically sang out, " Here, Lord, is un's." In accordance with her dignity as an old maid, she retained her seat until the gambolling children were out of her path, maiden-like preferring to go home alone.

Lydia's narration of Aunt Sallie's capture in Africa had thrilled me with a desire to hear the story from her own lips; so, when I asked her to tell me where she lived before she came to Green Forest, she chirpingly replied, " In de canebrake, in Wangpool."

" Where is that, tell me ? "

Picking up her bench, she motioned me to follow, mumbling, " Ole Sal hates board walls."

Behind the wash-house she led me ; then stopped in front of a bench used by house-servants when off duty. Here the winter sun shed its warmest rays.

The negroes wondered who had hammered the legs of this bench so deep into the earth. Marlborough declared he knew ; for he had " seen a no 'count yaller man makin' love to de nurse dere while de w'ite chilluns was playin'." On this matter Lydia kept her own council.

Aunt Sallie placed her stool in front of this bench, seated herself, lifting her feet on a level with her body. She then motioned me to take the other end of the seat.

Chuckling, she exclaimed, " Daught, you is a big gal; w'en I peeped at you in de nurs'ry you was sech a red rat! Why don't folks call you Sack?—dat's missus' name."

Lydia had tried to break her of the habit of speaking to us as " daught," but it was useless. " Massa an' missus hears un's call dem 'daught'; dey don't 'monstrate wid un's."

" Now ; how about your father and mother ? " I asked. " Did you leave them in Wangpool ? "

Huddling herself close beside me, she appeared to fear recapture, " Poo (pa)," she said, " he drink, dess caise de king's pen ware empty; he punch un's in de rib, 'You'll do.' Moo (ma) was cookin' rice, an' w'en she git a chance she filled a calabash : ' Here, run hide in de canebrake. Let poo see you an' de king'll swallow you whole.' De sun was a dippin' ober de cane-top " (she ducked her head into my lap as the scene seemed vividly recalled), "an' poo come a yellin' my name. Down ter de riber-side un's flopped behin' de young cane, quick, a white man slap un's in de facc, den pitch un's ober he shoulder, so,"—flirting her handkerchief across my shoulder.

I bounded out of my seat and on to my feet, sure that a bushy-bearded Hollander was about to capture me as well.

But Aunt Sallie, having recalled her past, felt she must complete the story :

" Un's an' lots of un's was pack in a big house a rockin' on de water. De boss com' an' toss 'longside of un's rice, but un's didn't want no eaten, caise un's inside was tumblin' out."

" How many weeks were you in the vessel, and where did the white man take you to ? " I asked.

With a deep sigh she answered : " Oh, it ware a long time, daught. Eb'ry day one of un's, stiff like a board, was pitched in de water. Un's wished it war un's."

Suspecting that she had been disembarked at some northern port, I inquired, " When you reached land where did you go ? "

She rose, and, hobbling on one foot, attempted to show how she walked when dragged out, her side, she said, bleeding : drawing her faded shawl about her, she chattered her toothless gums, giving, as she evidently desired, the idea of one suffering from a chill. " De sand was cold, it burned un's toes ; w'ite feathers like rain was droppin' from de moon."

Lifting one foot, then another, she chafed their bare soles. (She could not be induced to wear shoes.)

"Would you like to go back to the canebrakes in Wangpool?"

Realising that no present danger surrounded her, she leaned against the wash-house, perched her bare feet once more upon her stool and, in real camp-meeting style, clapped her hands, shouting, "Glory, glory, bless de Lord! Un's has plenty sun, plenty taters, plenty rice, an' a good boss. Bless de Lord! Glory, hallelujah! Samuel, wey is you? Here, Lord, is un's."

And Aunt Sallie understood the art of shouting, too, her rhythm of sound thrilling the soul of every one that ever heard her. When she "got religion," she doubtless was borne out of church on a door, showing no sign of life, save an occasional cry for mercy or a shout of exultation.

In spite of all the cruelties that have been depicted, there were many happy scenes on southern plantations. Certainly in Siberty county, where we lived. Unfortunately, however, it had to be vacated by the whites from May until November. For, notwithstanding the miasmatic feeding properties of the grey moss,—that curse of a southern clime,—fever and ague sometimes shook one from head to foot on the hottest

day in August. To avoid this, sixteen wealthy
planters settled a village in the pine land, calling
it Greenville, in honour of Green Forest's owner.
Summer residences dotted the streets, gay flower-
beds in front and vegetable gardens in the rear.
There was one Presbyterian church, in charge of
Midway's pastor, and also a school-house; but no
shop or store.

Children reared in Greenville recall vividly
floggings they had in its house of learning.
For the master declared that, as he was paid
to teach, he would see that "birds that could
sing and wouldn't sing, were made to sing."
And how he often flounced a boy, face down,
across a bench !—using freely an oaken paddle.

Father McCall, who taught this teacher, had,
it appears, set him a bad example. And after a
long and arduous life in pulpit and country school,
the aged clergyman had, as his sole earthly possessions, an old white horse, Bob, and a faithful
coloured man, Daniel. His declining years he
spent visiting among his former pupils. Our
parent was his favourite one—to judge from the
frequency of his visits. And the mere memory
of interminable hours of agony that ensued for
Letha and me, still revive apprehension. In fact,
whenever we recognised the jogging trot of old Bob
coming down the avenue, we fled,—if we could.

4

Father McCall, however, died at the age of eighty-three, at a neighbour's, in a room named Purgatory. Owing to his dislike for the old clergyman, whom he nevertheless had to entertain, the host had assigned him to this chamber.

Lydia was deeply impressed by this incident. The truth is, she had despised him for a long time for alway scolding "her children," who chanced to doze while he prayed for twenty minutes round our family altar. She also often thrilled us with accounts of his cruelty when in charge of a country school.

Indeed, according to Lydia's narration, Father McCall, in the eighteenth century, actually put an unruly boy under the loose slab of a brick grave,—birches having been broken over his shoulder without avail.

"Dat day," Lydia said, "the chilluns was all whisp'rin', wond'rin' if poor Stephens would be smothered. De dismissal bell had no sooner tapped dan de whole school rushed out an' on ter de grave ter see de daid boy. No boy was there, only a pile of loose earth wid a shoe-sole on top,—jes as if de skeleton had tossed de cum'brin' clay. 'He's daid!' de chilluns shouted; 'oh, where is Stephen?' It was den dat hardhearted man called out, 'Stephen, you rascal, come out o' dat hole!' Crawlin' backward from de tunnel he had dug de poor boy stood up as dirty as a pig, wid a tired, hongry look in his eyes."

This thrilling story was always told us when tucked in bed, followed by the injunction, " Chil-luns, go ter sleep ; it's late." One of Lydia's peculiarities was that she never forgot harrowing details.

On Sundays, sitting in a rear pew of Green-ville's church, she listened with rapt attention to Biblical accounts of hell-fire and brimstone.

Letha and I reaped the benefit of her reten-tive memory: when more inclined to play than sleep, we have spent agonising moments looking for red flashes beside our trundle-bed.

Sunday was a holy day in Greenville ; chins dropped two inches, and a really spread-mouth laugh was marked as an unpardonable sin. Horses were never harnessed ; coachmen, therefore, had sly opportunities for quiet flirtations.

Rows of cabins were built in the rear of the village-dwellings ; for house-servants and the con-valescent from our plantations.

Nights were merry over quilting-frames, where old women helped with the quilting ; coachmen, maids, and footmen standing by, threading needles.

Feede, Mr. Winn's cook, who was especially

clever, agreed to superintend the laying of a
quilt for Dean's seamstress. Wishing, then, to be
sure that everything was ready before quilting
began, she tucked her four-year-old son John in
bed, covered him head and ears, and hastened to
the quilting-bee.

But green plums and unripe peaches kept John
awake, and, notwithstanding his overburdened
but unsatisfied stomach, he stole out of bed, in-
tending to make his way to Dean's, in search of
a bite of quilting-supper. For "little pitchers
have big ears."   John then and there disappeared.

The quilt was finished, tightly rolled, and laid
aside. An hour before dawn, Feede rushed
home, hoping to get a wink of sleep before preparing her master's breakfast.

To her dismay she found her little girl Amy
alone under the blankets. From one cabin to another she rushed, asking, " Is you see dat rascal
of a nigger John? De black imp is quit my bed
an' gone de Lord knows where."

The negroes of the village, frightened and talking together in groups, concluded certain sounds
some one had heard, were the growls of the mate
of a big black bear killed the summer before
in Bulltown Swamp, a few miles away ; Its skin
now served as a door-mat, to the horror of some,

and to the amusement of other, small ones of the place.

After the sun rose, a footman put the black populace into a fever of excitement by declaring that he saw distinct foot-prints of a monster bear in the road opposite Mr. Winn's cottage.

Rushing to her master's room, Feede roused him with the startling news, that her boy John had been eaten "head an' foot" by a big black bear."

The men of the village were soon in their saddles, fully armed for a hunt in the swamp.

Not a vestige of John was found. And though Feede had often thrashed him, declaring he was "de wuss little rascal in Greenville, an' would some day git his desarts if he didn't men' his ways," she now appeared broken-hearted. For a new-made grave covers many faults.

Lydia, who was familiar with the adventures recorded in the "Young Marooners," determined to protect her household from the jaws of wild beasts. She therefore stripped an old red flannel petticoat into long bits, and tacked them about her cabin door and window, and each night she made sure that a pot of water boiled in the chimney-corner, with a tin ladle near by, so as to scald Bruin's eyes.

The servants were not the only ones excited

over this strange disappearance. Ladies, in ex-
changing visits, could talk of little else.

Greenville was built in the midst of a wide
extent of pine forest, where never a traveller
passed, and from which long ago the red man had
fled to the canebrakes of Florida.

In the nursery Lydia moaned, "If we could
only see dat w'ite scar on de poor daid John's
left arm."

Our summer retreat had no lack of snakes; a
few days of warm sunshine and out they crawled,
in new spring coats of many colours. We hung
their rusty discarded skins about Lydia's neck;
then she added them to the adornments of her
cabin, as " charms to keep 'way ghosts."

Mocking-birds, our southern nightingales, trilled
their softest love-notes from dawn till midnight : imitating the barking of dogs, mewing of
cats, and even the crying of children ; and the
last so effectively as to deceive mothers and
nurses. Near the dwellings they built their nests,
and their young were our household pets.

One morning, I remember, a cry of distress
hastened my father from the breakfast-room ; he
wondered what could ail one of the feathered
denizens of his home.

Cuddled in a warm nest, between the limbs of
a spikenard tree, were four bare-bodied birds,

hungry, and doubtless wondering why the early worm was not at hand. The mother-bird, in truth, was under the power of a monstrous rattlesnake coiled at the root of a spreading laurel-tree. From a wide to a narrowing circle she flew, uttering notes of distress, unable, however, to resist the fascinating eyes of the serpent, glistening above the coil. The tail protruded on the side, its chain of rattles constantly in motion. By a law of nature rattlesnakes cannot strike, and so eject poison, without first ringing bells as a warning.

Seeing that the power of the bird was waning, father fired his gun.

The smoke cleared away. We beheld a reptile six feet long, with twelve rattles and one button, making its age thirteen years.

Lydia danced with excitement, saying, " De horrid t'ing, day by day watchin' my chilluns at play. He had a taste of poor John's black fingers, I's sure, caise bears an' snakes is good friends."

IV.

Daddy Toby's Courtship,

"A damsel has ensnared him with the glances
Of her dark roving eyes, as herdsmen catch
A steer of Andalusia with a lasso."
                                LONGFELLOW.

A GORGEOUS Indian summer set in, as the season of sunshine and heated air waned. Peas and bean stalks were dry and withered. Relieving the death-like aspect here and there were poles covered with gay-blooming cypress vines, with crimson stars peeping from beneath the feathery green leaves. The cheek of apples and of quinces, too, had felt the kiss of the summer's sun, helping thus to redeem the look of desolation.

In the kitchen our cook Affie busied herself in preserving fruit for winter use; often nodding while her pot boiled. From her father, an Indian warrior, she inherited a fiery temper; still we delighted in playing tricks whenever she slept.

Finding her snoring one day, with her dress-front open, Letha caught a live toad, and bade me—ever her willing servant—drop it into Affie's bosom.

I had no sooner done so, than she picked up a lightwood knot, and, but for timely aid from Marlborough, all practical jokes for me would have been at an end.

From our parents we inherited a fondness for fun and frolic. Of course no one suspected our mother of playing tricks,—with her large family and numerous guests. Notwithstanding, she did play them ; and many. Lydia, too, was always her ready accomplice ; in fact, she would, with a face as serene as if sitting at the communion table, present a dish of night supper to a room full of girls preparing for bed, saying, " Wid de compliments of Mars John Castle an' his friends."

In truth, not one load of shot had been expended by any of the young men in killing the red-headed woodpeckers that were boiled in the bird pillau, prepared for a night-supper treat, their bitter and uneatable flesh impregnating every grain of rice.

Mother, at other times, regaled the boys with a platter of cakes well-lined with cotton wool. Girls and boys' declarations of innocence were, of course, never believed by either.

Evening entertainments were frequent at Green Forest. A very amusing one was when each young guest was robed in a sheet, with a pillow-case for turban ; suggestive of ghostly visitors but for rosy lips and laughing voices. However, no one was allowed to waltz or polka save with brothers or cousins.

It is true that the blue laws of Connecticut had long been abolished, but our parents were very strict. At the festivities held on our plantation, Daddy Toby and his string band supplied the music for dancing. Toby was the professor of love-making on the estate, coaching young men how to make known their feelings, and maids how to accept a proffered hand or heart.

In fact, Toby had mastered the science of love-making ; and he magnanimously employed his skill for the benefit of his race.

One of Green Forest's honored guests, Gerald Jones, being in sore distress, resolved to enlist the professor's aid. " Teach me, Toby," said he, " for my nights are nightmares of despair. My girl laughs when I swear she's the idol of my heart. I must convince her somehow that I adore her."

Surrounded by a merry group of young people, Toby tingled the strings of his banjo, and grinned from ear to ear.

" Boss, I can't teach w'ite folks ; it's only niggars needs larnin'."

Gerald's bosom-friend rushed to the supper-room, and returned with half a cake, snow-white, with sugar frosting. "Here, Professor, is your fee; payable at once. Let's have the lesson."

Toby claimed a fee for his services: a brace of partridges, a dozen eggs, a chicken, or possum.

The cake was not to be resisted. So, pulling himself together with a desperate effort, he scratched his kinky head, cleared his throat, half closed his eyes,—in clairvoyance style,—and gently twanged the treble strings of his instrument.

"Now, sah," said he, "put on your bes' Sunday-go-ter-meetin' clothes, parfume your nose-rag wid allegator's musk, comb your hair slick wid bear's grease, wash your face wid soft soap-suds; fer it must shine wid love bubblin' in your t'roat. Flirt your hick'ry stick, keepin' time wid your quick-beatin' heart" (indicating the same with his fiddle-bow). "Call at de young lady's house."

Thumping three times on the body of his banjo, he simulated the voice from within, "'Whose dar?'

"'De hon'rable Mr. Axson.'

"'Will de hon'rable Mr. Axson pull de latch-string an' com' in?' 'Good ev'nin', Miss. De

hon'rable Mr. Axson is tak' dis fav'rable chance
of payin' his 'spects ter de lovely Miss Dix.'—Be
sure you bows low.

"'Will de hon'rable Mr. Axson take a seat
an' be seated on de bench in de chimney-jamb?'
'T'ank you, my dear miss.'

" When you is crossed your legs, like w'ite folks,
pull out your han'kerchief ; wipe de bear's grease
from your forehead; blow your nose; den proceed, saying, 'A July sun is turnin' de corn-blades
ter windward, de water floodin' de rice-fields sends
de stalks galavantin' from side ter side ;' den, wid
a tender understandin', ask if de young lady is
been watchin' de cotton-sprouts, what de warm
sun makes grows, jes like love, 'fore you know it
dey is great bushes an' de fowls of de air comes
an' builds deir nest. 'Now, miss, has you notice
de moon rises later eb'ry quarter,—whisp'rin'
'cross de fire,—dat old prophets say de full moon
makes folks fall in love.' At dis moment you
must jump ter your feet wid an ecstasy, declarin'
dose larned men knew what dey was discoursin'
'bout, caise since de las' full moon de heart of
de hon'rable Mr. Axson is been burnin' ter cin-
ders. Dis is a convenient time fer plump your
bench close beside de gal cornered by de right
han' chimney-jamb. Your heart's a-beatin' lik' a
big drum ; it's a ticklish minute, but lean forward,

an' wid de impression of a preacher, whisper 'My dearest Miss Dix, is de hon'rable Mr. Axson's comp'ny 'ceptable so far dis eb'nin'?' (Gals likes ter count on fingers an' toes deir chances ter git married. Don't proceed widout a clue.) Tossin' her pretty head, she says, 'I ain't t'ought much 'bout it yet.'

"'Now, my lovely Miss Dix, bend your intelegent min' ter cogitate, caise Mr. Axson is mak' dis eb'nin' call wid de full purpose of 'dressin' you wid a cou'tship. Floppin' her han's over her sparklin' eyes, she sings out, so folks kin hear, 'Oh! Mr. Axson, you is com' fer mak' game of me.' Now's your chance! Drop on your knees, foldin' your finger-tips ober your heart hammerin' ginst de coat-front. Turn your eyes upward wid an ag'ny drippin' out de corners; say wid great impression, 'Lord bless your soul, my dear little miss, de sight of you dis eb'nin' is 'nough ter shake de heart of a lion. What you t'inks of a human bein'? I's been a commissioner fer ladies dis twenty years, an' no young lady is eber before bring Mr. Axson mind ter compose till you has dis eb'nin'. I'd rather have a kiss from your rosy mouth dan t'irty pieces of silver.'

"Gals makes it a p'int of bein' shy de furs night. But keep your courage; don't be coward. You is sow'd de seed; let de peach season in de brandy. Make a move ter go home an' watch how Miss Dix hates fer see you leavin'.

" Your hickory under your armpits, your stove-pipe on de back of your head, lean ober, an' when shakin' hands say : ' If de hon'rable Mr. Axson's comp'ny is anyway 'ceptable ter Miss Dix, he'll call ag'in at another time an' mak' a call ' ; put your hot lips on de knuckles of Miss Dix's right paw. Niggers is used to cuffin'—you may git a real love blow 'long side your nose."

Toby's thoughts prompted action, and he accordingly made a low bow to Gerald, who had stood prominently forward while receiving his instructions. The old man then picked up the frosted cake, and bounded out of the room before any one recovered from their surprise, leaving his banjo and hat behind. Search proved unavailing ; for he was doubtless behind a live-oak tree in the dark storing away the cake, before the honorable Miss Dix, that was, could get hold of it.

Considerable shrewdness is woven into this stereotyped, parrot-like form of a cornfield negro's courtship.

I have written it verbatim, but the main harmony and music of it is lost in not hearing it intoned by untutored lips.

Gerald Jones, with this fair start, was able to conclude his love-making.

Toby voiced the opinion of the plantation, when he declared that, " Had Molbro been properly instructed his pie would never have turned to dough "; while Scipio declared, " It was alway so wid hot-headed, pompous mens holdin' a pair of carriage-lines, t'inkin' dey had more sense, even 'bout love-makin', dan odder folks ; any blind man could see dat Molbro was caught in briar brambles—married to one 'oman an' groanin' for anodder man's wife." He summed up by saying, " Take heed, young mens an' 'omens, take heed ; massa is give me 'structions, an' I's goin' ter force dem at de p'int of dis whip,"—which then emitted a shrill, popping sound. " Men an' 'omens be warned, 'specially ag'in free yaller niggars."

V.

Machiah Baptised.

"That all-softening, overpowering knell,
The tocsin of the soul—the dinner-bell."
BYRON.

WHEN we gave place to newcomers in the nursery, Lydia told to our successors the story of a dainty supper enjoyed years before by a Bulltown Swamp bear and a rattlesnake.

And from time to time she, with cabalistic signs and enigmatic looks, invoked the aid of supernatural spirits to keep order. The most fiery temper would soon be quelled, as the youngster was ever eager to listen to her mysterious narrations. With Toby, she was convinced that all graveyards were full of live ghosts, popping up o' nights, like Jack o' Lanterns.

Few negroes, in fact, would pass Midway cemetery, or any other one, after dark. Compelled to do so, they turned their pockets wrongside out.

The alternate preachers at Pleasant Grove church in vain warned their congregations not to believe in ghosts; it was unworthy of a true Christian faith! At best, however, we are but frail mortals, prone to stumble. And so Parson Lee reflected one night when returning, on horseback, from a deathbed. As he reached Midway cemetery he reined in his weary horse, peering among the dimly-outlined graves. For the ensuing Sunday's sermon a suitable text recurred to his mind, and was audibly repeated: " Arise, ye righteous! Come to judgment!"

To his horror, from behind a vaulted sepulchre, came a reply clear and distinct, " Yea, Lord, I'm coming." His mare, urged by rusty spurs, galloped home. But next Lord's day the preacher's text was *not* " Arise, ye righteous!"

Lydia was not alone in her fondness for ghostly narrations; workers in cotton and corn-fields were constantly repeating new yarns, mingled with gossip. Interest seemed now to be centred on the frequency of Marlborough's visits to Professor Joe Lamont's place,

James, being a fisherman, he could come to his wife only from Saturday until Monday.

Marlborough accompanied his master on business trips, and as he was well versed in the news of the day, Lydia was often seen in close talk

with him. But, though only gratifying her inquiring turn of mind, her action was stigmatized
as a flirtation with her former lover.

One great amusement to her was the arrival of
negroes, bought at auction marts.

As a girl, she had experienced the excitement,
and now when three blasts of the plantation
bugle assembled the field negroes for the ceremony of an introduction, she was always on the
outskirts of the crowd with her " w'ite chilluns."

Scipio, the foreman, conducted to the front
Cæsar, a fine-looking negro man, with his wife
Molly and his daughter Peggy.

As was his custom, my father then introduced
them ; adding, " Cæsar, you and your family have
come to work among us.   I'm sure my people will
give you a welcome."   With a merry twinkle in
his eyes, he turned to a group of young men :
" Cracow, Stephney, Cyrus, you marriageable
fellows, come forward.   Let me present Peggy !
It's about time we were having a marriage-feast,
don't you think?   I've a fatted calf, and I'm
sure we would all enjoy a slice of wedding-cake.

Peals of laughter ensued, and scores of fingers
pointed in the direction of an overgrown youth,
six feet in his shoes. " Massa, ain't you take
notice how slick dat boy Cracow combs his wool?"
asked one old man. " Don't you see him eb'ry

day helpin' Chloe hoe he row? We is all on us groanin' fer a bite of w'ite cake."

"Cracow and Chloe, step to the front," said my father. "I'll decide how you'll suit before giving my consent."

Cracow appeared, proudly touching his fore-lock; he looked wistfully in the direction of a group of women; but Chloe was nowhere to be seen: she was crouching behind her companions.

"You have my blessing, Cracow," continued my father. "Remember, women need a bit of coaxing. "Scipio, give Cæsar and his family the double house, number twenty-five."

A small, thickset man, with wife and three young children, was next announced.

"Machiah, you are now on a plantation where kindness will be shown you. I bought you, determined to allow you a chance to turn over a new leaf and so make a man of yourself, and I'm sure these, my people, will help you. Do your work, and you'll find no cause for complaint here."

"Dat you won't," happy voices sang out. If you neber had a good master in Floridy, you's got one now!"

"Thank you!" And, with a smile, my father lifted his hat, showing a noble white forehead.

Machiah's scowl turned to a grin: "My new

massa, I's goin' ter do my best, but ole man
Wiley beat me so, my back was sore de most on
de time."

Again a chorus of voices spoke: " Do your
work, brudder, an' you'll hav' no sore back on
Green Forest."

With uncovered head Frank, noting his opportunity, bowed to his master ; and then, turning to
Machiah, he pointed to Peter's crowing cock.
" Come to dat chu'ch, brudder, deir de Holy
Speret teches de innards. I's see lots of niggers
no 'count tel de Speret flies at dem, sayin' Stop !
sinner ! stop !"

Lydia and "her children " huddled together for
protection from his startling words and gestures.
" Stop, I say. Sinner, you may dance up dat
broad road, but dose lights is a blazin' from a
volcano, an' w'en it bu'st out, 'you'll hurry an'
scurry only ter fall ober de Niag'ra where t'under
roars an' de sun of rej'icin' is gone down, de moon
turned ter blood. In dat chu'ch a sweet word is
callin', ' Don't be fread ! com' ter me. I de Lord
kin still de storm. Peace be yourn.' "

The   crowd   responded,   "Amen ! Amen !"
listening so attentively as not to note the suppressed smile on their master's face, who turned
to Scipio, saying, "Give Machiah house number
twenty."

A thrifty woman, who, on Sunday nights, occasionally treated her family to a fried fowl, occupied the adjoining cabin.

One Monday morning she lodged her complaint: "Massa, de young rooster was done ter a turn, an' I stepped out de front dooe ter call Bob an' de chilluns; w'en I goes ter sarve up dat chicken, dey was only de empty fryin' pan a frizzlin'. We track de grease outside de back dooe an' nobody is eat dat fowl but dat no 'count niggar Kiah."

In truth, it was a week before Machiah was seen, his wife declaring she didn't know where he had gone.

When the store-room was opened to give weekly rations, on Saturday night, Machiah came in his turn. "Massa," he said, "please, sah, scuse me dis time; I couldn't help it, sah. But if you'll scuse me I is neber goin' in de woods ag'in."

Without a word of reproof, his master looked at him. With a kindly but troubled face, he then turned to Scipio, saying, "Give him his meat, peas, potatoes, and corn-meal. I promised to allow him a fair chance to do better."

However, scarcely a day thereafter but some complaint arose and was lodged against Machiah.

Frank, as watchman, strove to do his duty, and prayed earnestly at the weekly meetings: "O

Holy Speret ! Fold d'y wings ober de eyes of dat
rampant sinner sleepin' in de hedges an' by-
ways. Wid dy mighty power lead him blin' fold
ter de t'rone of grace, whey is bounteous
pardon."

From bench to bench rose " Amen ! Amen ! "

Scipio fingered his " cotton planter," strapped
across his shoulders,—an insignia of his rank !

Machiah evidently felt the jeers of his fellow-
labourers more than he did his master's reproofs;
and by a mere accident, a new turn was given to
the usual mode of punishment.

Three blasts of the bugle brought the people
together again, many having in their hands long
switches. With a tone of sadness my father
spoke :

" Stand to the front, those of you who have
been cutting my young trees. Scipio, file them
into two lines, six feet apart."

Lydia wondered whatever was to pay.

Walking up to Machiah, my father continued,
" Here are twenty men and women who can prove
that you, Machiah, have stolen from them ; and,
though your master admitted to me that you
would occasionally sleep in the woods, I brought
you to this comfortable home, believing kindness
would make you a better man. Frank has urged
you to go to church, and offered prayer for you,

but it has done no good ; my young fellows will soon be following your bad example. Now then, pull off your jacket and walk up and down between this line. Let those you have wronged punish you. Don't run. Any one of these men will lay hold of you before you have gone ten steps. Pull your jacket off ; I am in earnest."

"Massa, do lick me yourself! Let Uncle Scipio t'rash me ; but don't let dem niggars hit me."

"No. It's from them you have stolen. Pull your jacket off. If this does no good, then I must sell you."

The march began between bristling switches, Hetty's birch whistling to the tune of a frying fowl, the bones of which had been found under the culprit's bed.

As father turned to go, he said, "Don't let me sound another bugle call for undress parade."

"Massa, you'll not blow no bugle for me ag'in, caise I is done made up my mind fer turn ober dat new leaf, an' I is goin' ter chu'ch, sah."

"All right ; that's the way to talk! Do your work and stay at home, leaving other folks' chickens and eggs alone, and you'll be treated kindly."

In giving his usual report some weeks after, Frank said :

" Massa, de Speret is touch Kiah wid de p'int
of he wing.   De odder night de bell hadn't done
clappin' when dat runaway nigger walk in de
sacred edifice, an' ter-day at Pleasant Grove chu'ch
Parson Lee put Kiah under de creek water,—
some folks say two inches deeper dan odders.
He spit de water out he mouth, shoutin', Bless
de Lord, my sin is washed away !   Bless de Lord
an' my good massa.'   Parson Lee say de word dat
dem what turn dey back on sin trustin' de Lord,
is neber gwine ter be disapp'inted.   Last week,
when dem boys laugh at Kiah, askin' if he ain't
tired sleepin' in a house, an' was fowl-meat sweet,
I speaks a kind word : ' Brudder, don't mind what
dem rampant sinners say, hold your mind 'umble-
like, pray de Lord, an' he'll keep you in de
narrow path.   I's hear dat de debil tempted de
Lord heself ; but he plant he foot on de rock, an'
no wind Satan could blow could move him from
de firm foundation.   Ain't dat so, massa ? "

" Yes.   The Bible says if we serve the Lord
with an honest heart, He will not forsake even
the vilest sinner.   The prodigal son, you know,
was met by his father, who killed for him the
fatted calf, although he had spent all his money
in riotous living.   Frank, I have noticed you
preach too much about hell-fire.   Next Sunday
take for your text, Love—' God is love.'   Come

on Saturday afternoon, and one of your young
missies will read what the Bible says about
Love."

"T'ank you, massa, fer de good cheer. It's
like de oil flowin' ober Aaron's beard, a reachin'
ter de hem of he coat. Sometimes I wishes I
could spell. Mars Flem' is teach me c-a-t cat, r-a-t
rat, but my head gits suffused. I says, 'Frank,
you's got a good memery, 'pend on dat.' Bro'
John's studyin', but after he's been bowin' ober
de book, he slams de speller on de floor. Boys,'
says he, 'you may talk 'bout readin' an' spellen,
but it's de hardest day's work my han's is sot ter
dis long time; de sweat rolls; hoein' in de August
sun don't bring out sech suffusion. Boys, you
may hav' de fedder an' speller, giv' me de ax an'
hoe.'"

My father continued: "There's another thing,
Frank. When you preach of love, you must
show it in your life, keeping your own lamp
trimmed and burning. Sinners may often be led
with a web of kindness, when they couldn't be
driven with scourges. Tell your people of green
bay trees, and of the cedars of Lebanon, where
Christ as a. Shepherd tends His sheep. Have
you never seen old Sawney lead my flocks from
one pasture to another with a handful of salt?
I wonder if you really love to preach?

"Massa, it's my glorification ter preach; ain't dere a word what says scatter de seed broadcast, fling it ober de great congregation; a stray bird may pick up a grain or two. Some takes root in shaller groun', an' jes as you is 'bout ter cut down dat yaller blade, de spring rains comes, dat corn pops up, an' fore you knows it dere is de shock; den de ripe corn in de ear. It's so wid dat run-away nigger: he seed de love in your eye when you tell Uncle Scipio ter give him meat, peas, potatoes, an' meal, aldo not a lick of work had he done. You showed him de handful of salt,—an' den between dose line of switches you cast a net round 'bout de camp of Israel; caise dat bery night he come ter de Gospel house o' prayer. From dat time we giv' Kiah de right hand o' fellowship, an' neber ceased ter pray dat he would git into de ark of safety. Las' Sunday when I ask all penitents ter come forward, he walk plumb ter de front of de pulpit an' drop on he knees. A hallaluyah rise in de air. De angel Gabriel must a heard de shouts of rej'icin.' I had been holdin' forth a solid hour. Seein' me dry in de mouth, de chu'ch sisterens sing out, 'Pull fer de shore, brudders, pull.' Folks don't count much on 'omens in chu'ch, caise de Bible says it's not fer 'omens to speak aloud in de house of God; but I notices dey is alway ten in de seats ter eb'ry

one man, an' dey don't snore like de mens ; nod-
din' deir head in real 'omen style. No voice sings
so clear, ' Heaven bells a-ringin', my soul engage.'
De menfolks waits outside de dooe a finishin'
dere pipe. Bro' Jack, who is my right-hand staff,
says ' Fellows, go in, you'll lose de p'int of de
'course.'

" My speret gits low when dey comes in late.
Satan whispers, ' Set down, Frank, dey is los' de
early dew ; it's no use ter preach any longer.' "

" Surely you don't give up so easily ? Cast
your bread upon the waters ! Perhaps, after
many days, it may return to you, and be sweeter
than the honeycomb.' "

" Dat's so, massa. I's goin' ter try de new gospel you tell me 'bout. I'll fling de flag o' love
ober my congregation an' see how many will 'list
under de banner."

" Tell your people also, Frank, how ' God so
loved the world that He gave His only begotten
Son to die for their salvation.' "

" It's so, massa. Folks don't like ter hear 'bout
fire an' parched tongues ; dey likes a easier road,
what don't 'quire hard rowin'. It ware so wid
Kiah. Bro' Jack an' me used ter warn him dat
he was standin' on de walls of Jericho. When
de t'ird blast blow, look out, brudder, dat you
ain't civered with brick an' mortar. But Kiah

give answer: ' I ain't on no wall, an' I's neber see a fence yit but if I's a mind ter I kin climb ober. I ain't comin' in chu'ch ter hear 'bout hell-fire. My back burn 'nough down in Floridy.'

" When we fling him dis word, ' Come ter me in de ark of safety, come, if you's tired, I'll give you rest, caise I de Lord is done all de work,' den he sing out, ' Here, Lord, is me.' "

" Frank, it was a kind word that won him at last. And so, in the same way, I try to make my people love me. We want no Uncle Toms, chained and bleeding, on Green Forest. I would pull down every fence, turn cattle to graze in the grain-fields, rather than have my work done with Scipio's " cotton planter " constantly in use. In your families there are times when punishment becomes a duty to your children. Riseburg has its court-house and police; public offenders are there dealt with by the law. On my plantation *I* must fill these positions, and it is not always easy to keep peace and order. You remember how my good and faithful coachman came near killing the mason Marmaduke? We must all exercise patience, keeping our hearts right before God."

" Dat's so, massa. No work is worth doin' if de soul ain't dere. No hallelujahs, no songs, kin rise ter de heav'nly choir. Don't git discouraged, massa, caise when de big book is open I's sure deir will be a word of rej'icin' fer you an' missus; a crown fer both on you. You is done de bes' you could fer we niggars, an' it will be writ down fer Christ's sake, too." ·

"Thank you, Frank. When the Lord sits upon His Throne, judging if there is a crown for you and me, we will cast it at His feet, saying, 'Not unto us, not unto us, but unto Him who gave His life that we might live.'"

"Dat we will, massa, dat we will! Praise de Lord; glory, hallelujah!"

VI.

A Gold=Marked Wedding Ring.

"Pity's akin to love."
THOMAS SOUTHERNE.

NOW it was, that a sudden and overwhelming sorrow overtook Lydia; her husband and three other men, while fishing, were overtaken by a furious gale, that capsized the boat. Only one man reached shore. He told how James and his companions went down, never more to rise.

Lydia moaned and wept, her mind meanwhile overawed by the dreadful accident that made her four piccaninnies orphans. Her " w'ite chilluns " soothed and petted her, but salty drops ran like rain down her dusky cheeks.

Marlborough drove the disconsolate widow and her children to Pleasant Grove the ensuing Sunday, where the funeral services were held. Dr. C. C. officiated, and inasmuch as he taught the doctrine of predestination, it was of course the foreordained will of God that James should lie in a watery grave.

Lydia wore a black calico dress, with a snow-white bandanna deeply bordered with black. Her children were also robed in emblems of mourning. Our "mommer" was a great favourite in the community, therefore the church was packed with people from our own and adjoining plantations, come to " de funeral wid no corpse."

More than one old woman gave her head a significant shake, saying, " Dat wife Flora, ober at Massa Joe's, had better keep her house in order, else her husband will quit altogedder. Mens is such queer kind o' folks ; dey is neber content, t'inking somebody else's peach is got a finer bloom dan de one dey has in hand."

During the time of this fresh sorrow, Marlborough, as one of the house-servants, deemed it his duty to console the lonely widow, who was breaking her heart with grief. So, his evening duties finished and a hush of repose spread over the estate, he sat on Lydia's cabin-steps or beside her chimney-corner.

" Dry your tears, Lyddy ; fer aldo the billows is gone ober James, God's will must be done ; some day it will come right. I know, my dear lady, de sun is set red, like blood, but wait patient, den when de clouds is all blowed over, de mornin' sky will shine, clear an' bright, an' you'll forgit de howlin' blast. I's goin' ter do all I kin fer you an' your orphans. Do try an' be happy. It breaks my heart ter see you weepin' dose salty tears."

Marlborough felt that this woman needed consolation far more than his wife needed his weekly visits. Flora, accordingly, waited in vain for her husband, knowing well the cause of his absence. But, woman-like, she hid the thorn that pierced deeper and deeper into her heart, and appeared to take little heed of idle gossip in the cornfields; if anything, boasting more than ever of her fine wedding-ring, " havin' a gol' mark half 'cross de inside."

But while Marlborough expended his best efforts in wiping away tears, a scene happened in his wife's house that influenced his whole after-life.

A coloured man of learning, it appears, stopped at Lamont's place to have a bite of supper with Flora's brother. While the hoe-cake was browning in the oven, he sat before the fire, showing a gold ring he was to put, the next Saturday night, on " de marriage finger of de likeliest gal over at Barnard's landin'."

" Is it got de gol' mark inside, like mine ?" and Flora handed over hers for him to appreciate its genuineness.

Slowly he spelt "L y d i a—Lydia."

Dropping skillet and corn-loaf, amazed and indignant, Flora snatched her ring and dashed it into the fire. With angry tones she screamed, "Is dat de gol' mark? Law! I'd neber a-wore it wid dat no count niggar's name had I a-knowd. When Flora puts on a ring ag'in it's got ter have 'Flora' writ inside."

Her brother hurriedly took the golden hoop from the bed of coals, dropping it on the hearth to cool.

Pointing disdainfully to it, Flora asked: "Is de name burnt out? Sure an' fer certain I'll neber tech it ag'in. I'll kick it so—behin' dose logs, an' let it turn ter ashes. Dere, let dat hateful man s'arch fer it; he'll neber find it."

Southern plantations were independent of even post-bags in those days, having, instead, a system of their own by which news flew,—not always correct in detail, I confess.

Marlborough heard early Monday morning, then, that his youngest child Flora had fallen into the fire; so, gaining permission to leave the plantation, he hurried to his wife's house. But he found it empty. He then sought the sufferer in the day nursery, from which a group of "blackies" ran to meet him, screaming, "Dey is Flora's pa comin'."

6

Lifting his child into his arms, he asked, "Is you fall in de fire, my little gal?"

"No, sah, ma licks me if I goes too close in de chimney-corner."

Leaving her soup pot, old Granny came to the door, mopping her sweltering face with the corner of her apron.

"How is this, Granny? Word came ter Green Forest dat my little Flora had fallen in de fire; here she is as spry as a kitten; massa will t'ink I told a lie."

"Ha! ha! It's dat wife of yourn foolin' wid fire, ridin' a high horse 'bout some nonsense writ in de ring she says is finer dan odder folks. Granny is had dis gol' ban' on her finger nigh on ter forty years an' no fuss is ris over it yit."

Troubled in mind, Marlborough returned to his wife's house, wondering who could have spelt out his secret. It was the dinner hour, and Flora arrived from the field.

With sarcasm in her voice, she accosted her husband: "Dat's you, a! Well, take yourself back; I's made up my mind ter have nothin' more ter do wid you. I is had 'nough of your nonsense. Go an' court dat fool-niggar Lyddy, fer all I cares. I kin marry lots of odder mens better dan you is."

They had often quarrelled before, so Marlborough went on arranging a shelf, not deigning to give a reason for his untimely visit. He noted, however, that there was no ring on his wife's finger.

"You is a 'ceitful fellow! You's brag 'bout dat big gol' mark, but I is done found out it's dat nasty mean 'oman Lyddy's name inside my ring. Liars is ketched up wid; dey says folks kin steal, but de bag'll be found some time. I's got you cornered now."

" If dat ring don't suit you, Flora, give it ter me an' stop your jawin'."

"Hah! hah! I ain't got your old brass. I's pitch it in de fire! Here, you kin s'arch fer it,"—handing him a hickory stick that always stood beside the chimney-corner—"brass don't melt so quick as gol'."

He turned over and over the ash-heap, but failed to find the golden hoop. Flora muttered to herself, " I always did say dat 'oman Lyddy was no kind o' 'count; she's got her finger in her missus' eye. She's a mean, nasty hussy."

Starting to his feet, her husband scowled, saying, "Shut your mouth, miss, or I'll shut it fer you;" then he lifted the hickory stick. "Let me hear you call dat name ag'in an' I'll slap your jaws. We nurse is as pure as de angels, an' so long as I's name Molbro no man or 'oman shall speak ag'in her."

"Slap on!" she enjoined, tilting her cheek to one side. "I has my t'oughts all de same. It 'pears to me your pure angel grows a pow'ful black pair o' wings."

"Take care dat your own life ain't spotted. You huntin' fer tips on odder folks' wings! I is sure if you'd heard sech talk 'bout freedom an' house-maids as Lyddy heard, you w'd have run away from your master. De stain of sin what befell we nurse at Green Forest is all wiped out, an' I tell you ter-day she's de best 'oman dat ever set foot on God's earth, white or black."

"When mens lays sech store by 'omens dat don't belong ter dem, you may be sure deir life is deep-spotted."

"Mens is not spected ter be angels. In Miss Chim's picture-books it's ladies what has gossamer wings an' is angels of love. Dose dressed in red, like debils, is mens, jes sech rascals as dat free niggar what tipped we nurse's wings wid black. If I had a smashed his face de firs' day, instead of de las', all dis trouble wouldn't be breakin' my heart."

"You needn't break your heart; your red an' yaller debil is gone to Savernake; shark fish is feed on James. Go, marry your black angel wid

white-spotted wings—you has my consent. I's
made up my mind you needn't bother ter come
here ag'in."

Little Flora sprang to her father's side at this
exciting moment. "Don't slap ma!—it hurts a
pow'ful lot."

Marlborough, who had a tender heart, unwound
his little girl's arm, and stepped outside the door.
"If it wa'n't fer dese chilluns of mine, I'd neber
darken de portal of dis cabin ag'in."

On his homeward way bitterness consumed his
mind. He returned, however, in time to take his
master's reins.

"I hope your child wasn't badly burned?"

"T'ank you, massa, my little Flora didn't fall
in de fire."

"How came the news, then?"

"Massa, kin I tell you de truth? My wife
Flora is a-kickin' up her heels 'bout de ring I give
her de night we was married; she say it ain't gol',
but brass, an' she pitch it in de fire."

Has she just discovered that her ring is brass?
It's seven years since you were married!"

It's not de quality troublin', it's a word inside
what's mak' dis fuss an' tarrification."

"A wedding-ring should have a word of
love."

"I bought it de time you was in Savernake

talkin' wid dat free niggar what is upset all my
life."

You were in love with our nurse, Lydia, then,
were you not ? "

" I was, massa; an' she was smilin' an' dancin' wid
me ; so I t'ought ter buy de ring.   De store-keeper
say w'ite folks have deir gals' name inside, an' if
I'd pay two bits he'd write it so soap an' water
wouldn't wash it out.   He write Lyddy.   All was
goin' well till dat free niggar set foot on we plantation."—He heaved a deep sigh.—" I's married,
massa, but dey neber will be dat warmin' toward
Flora like what burns fer Lyddy.   If I had only
stopped ter t'ink before dat marriage-deed was
done ober at Massa Joe's !   Nobody know'd 'bout
dat name in my ring.   Flora t'ought it was de
gol' mark, till last Sunday night a black man what
could read, spell out Lyddy.   In a minute Flora
kicked at de ring sendin' it behin' de fire an' now
she's a-spreadin' out her min', callin' we nurse
dreadful names ; an' she don't know ter dis day
'bout de gol' mark inside.   Massa, ain't we nurse
got de best character of any black person in Siberty County ? "

" I thought you had a good wife, Marlborough—
your clothing and that of your children show the
care of an attentive mother."

" Flora's handy wid her needle, sah, an' kin

cook a pot of gumbo equal ter Aunt Affie, but mendin' clothes an' eaten is not all a man looks fer when he goes home. Dere is no intercourse o' mind dere like what I feels fer Lyddy. Even de Angel Gabriel heself couldn't shet he eyes ter we nurse's beauty. W'ite folks breaks up marriages when dey sells niggars. Massa, won't you untie dat knot what binds me ober at Massa Joe Lamont's? Den, massa kin I court we nurse?"

Turning squarely round, eyeing his coachman, my father replied, "You are talking rashly. Remember, you, of your own free will, asked permission to marry Flora; and when Dr. C. C. said, 'Will you love her so long as life lasts,' you replied ' I will, sir.' Then he said, ' Whom God has joined together let no man put asunder.' You, Marlborough, are my slave. But no master has a right to break the marriage-vow. I'm sorry to hear you are not happy, but you must abide by your choice; had you not been hasty, Juno might have called you Pa, instead of James."

Dat's so, massa. My pie is turned ter dough; my harp's a-hangin' on a willer tree. If James had come back ter tell 'bout dat wat'ry grave, I might hav' kep' my heartache down, but de upturnin' of dat boat is set Lyddy free, an' dose billows is toss up an' hit me plumb on my breast ag'in. You reads in de Bible 'bout marriages made in heaven. Is dat 'cordin' ter de law, fer me ter buy a ring fer one 'oman I loves better dan myself, den somehow it got put on Flora's finger ? "

" You put it on yourself ; it was your own do- ing, not by command of God or man. There, take this money, go to old man Dunham's, in Riseburg, and buy a real gold ring for Flora. Let me hear no more.

" T'ank you, massa, I'll do my best over at Mars Joe's fer please you, sah ; caise nobody ever had a better master dan me an' Lyddy is got ; if only Flora would stop talkin' 'bout black wings, when we nurse is as pure as de w'itest w'ite folks."

Flora asked, on receiving the new ring, " Has it got Flora inside ? "

" No ! I is had 'nough of writin' names. Niggars gits mystified apein' w'ite folks. De Lord made deir skin different an' He 'lowed dey better hav' deir own ways an' consequences."

" Wid black faces can't dey wear gol' ? " Is dis brass ? "—fitting it on her marriage-finger.

" Don't ask me dat word ; I's tired hearin' your talk. I is done my best. If you ain't satisfied, hand me my ring, an' I'll quit Lamont's place. Green Forest is good 'nough fer me or any black man."

"All right, go 'long wid you ; but you won't hav' your chilluns, I kin tell you."

"Don't be too sure ; my master's pockets is full o' money."

"Jes prezactly like you. Caise you has a good boss, nobody else has. Mars Joe is a grand professor, but inside his vest front a heart big as a meetin' house thumps. Put your jews-harp ober de door-sill, you'll neber play it fer dat boy o'yourn nowhere but right here. By de bye, tell me is your black angel changed de mournin' head handkerchief fer red an' yaller? Is she lookin' fer anodder husband ter give ter shark fish?"

"Flora, I came here wid a peace-offerin', an' like a decent black man has offered it ter you ; but you ain't satisfied, you keeps on harpin' 'bout wings tipped wid black. I 'lows most everybody's wings, no matter how w'ite dey is, has black spots. Is you certain no jet-black fedders is in yourn? Is you neber sinned?"

No answer. Then Marlborough bade his wife good-bye. "I's going home where I's content, aldo my heart aches a pow'ful lot."

He, whose heart was more like lead than flesh, on reaching Green Forest, at once sought the woman uppermost in his thoughts.

Regardless of Toby's stereotyped form of expression, he grasped her black hands.

"Lyddy, I is fight ag'in my own mind; has beat my breast till my soul is in my shoe-tips; but it's no use; a man's a man an' you can't turn him to a lam'. I took a new peace-offerin' ter Flora, but it's no good; she keeps jawin' 'bout you havin' your fingers in missus' eyes. Oh, go wid me, Liddy, an' let us get down on our knees an' beg her ter 'nul dat contrac' ober at Massa Joe's what I make in a hurry. Den, Lyddy, will you be mine? You knows I love you better dan de apple of my eye, I has neber loved anybody else. Make me happy. Be my wife dis very night."

"Bro' Molbro,"—and her voice trembled with emotion,—"don't talk so ter me. I never forgits how my life is stained wid sin by dat yaller free niggar; but I is been ter de Lord fer pardon, an' Mars C. C. says Christ kin' wash out de deepest stain of sin. Would you blacken my name ag'in? You 'bused an' almost killed Marmaduke; now you are followin' him step by step." Rising, she motioned him away: "Go, go! De Lord helpin' me, massa an' missus will neber turn me out of de nurs'ry ag'in fer bein' unworthy o' their trust. You would pollute my happy married life an' make my sorrow turn ter fresh weepin'? Go! Be true ter Flora, an' if she keeps on talkin' 'bout my black wings, tell her I must suffer fer my own sin. I'm not ashame', Bro' Molbro, dat I did love you once. But now you belongs ter Flora. In heaven, when we meet, we kin walk arm in arm, washed from sin, an' married 'fore God."

VII.

Robin Decides to Marry.

"The Gods are wonderous kind."

IN one of the cabins for convalescent workers, Lucy died suddenly, leaving six small children. She was wife to Robin and sister of our seamstress, Lily.

Frank tried to console the husband, who bitterly rebelled against God for taking his wife, leaving Flora to his brother Marlborough, who took little trouble to visit her.

"I suppose, Bro' Frank," snapped the disconsolate man, " dat's de flag of love you flings over your congregation! It's de banner you wants us ter 'list under! When you kin splain why I is left wid a lot of mudderless chilluns, 'abreakin' my heart over Lucy's grave, I'll com' ter church,— not before."

"I's not a profit, an' can't splain all de Bible words," said Frank, " but don't deride dem ; chilluns was eat up once caise dey derided de old profit."

" You needn't fret, preacher, I'll not be snatched up like de boy John, at Bulltown swamp."

Winter rains had pattered over new-made graves, after which cotton and corn sprouted into life under the influence of spring days. Lucy's mound, then, was green with young grass-blades.

The cloud of sorrow overhanging Robin's home day after day seemed less dark, when he avowed his intention of supplanting the dead woman's place with another wife " 'fore de corn was in de tassel." With an eye to business, he ingratiated himself with the women, calling them " ladies " in place of "hunna people,"—the plantation parlance for "you people."

" Ladies, stand fer your rights," he insisted ; " an' most of all, don' take a gol' ring wid a big gol' mark inside. Folks says dat sister-in-law of mine ain't a-consarnin' herself 'bout what's goin' on at Green Forest. Jes t'ink a man wid his wife three miles away an' he not botherin' ter go dere. If it was ten miles I'd go ter my Lucy, an' swim a creek beside. No wonder Flora kicked her weddin' ring in de fire."

Leaning upon his hoe-handle, Toby, professor of love-making, voiced the opinion of the men, when he said that the coachman did quite right to use the ring he had. " Folks mustn't be hard on

Bro' Molbro. When he found his love-knot had come loose, he hadn't de heart ter pay money fer anodder gol' band. Who would have thought Liddy would fool a fellow! But gals will be gals; dey like high airs an' fine dressin'; never stoppin' ter ask how big a rascal is inside de sto'-clothes. In de fust place, if Bro' Molbro hadn't been so larned in his own mind, an' had a-given me a new pipe wid a bundle o' tobacco, fer fee, de hon'rable Mrs. Cummins might ter-day a bin de hon'rable Mrs. Molbro Janes; but mens is mens, an' I's conclude one-half of dem is fools."

In the meantime, Robin became impressed with the need of offering his sister-in-law a bit of Christian advice. His fellow-workers tried to dissuade him, saying :

"You'd best 'tend ter your own business at Green Forest; ain't dere a lot of likely 'omens here? Folks often gits dere toes burned a warm-in' dem at some odder man's fireplace."

However, he asked permission to visit at Professor Joe Lamont's. And his master, suspecting that he was in search of a wife, gave him a pass covering a month's time.

No negro in slavery days could leave his owner's estate without a written order. Found without this pass, he made himself liable to corporal pun-ishment at the hand of the country patrol.

Her brother-in-law's unexpected call greatly pleased Flora; for, despite her outward cheerfulness, she was a lonely woman and hourly longed to forget and forgive her many quarrels with her husband.

She put on her table the best her cupboard offered; and spoke tenderly to Robin of dead Lucy. Once or twice she sarcastically referred to a pair of spotted wings and a black head handkerchief worn by a woman at Green Forest. But her visitor was engrossed with the hog and hominy in his tin plate. She spread a pallet for the night in front of the fire.

At break of day she rose to brew a cup of coffee for Robin before he returned to work.

"Molbro may not be content here, my lady," said her visitor, "but I is, if you'll accept o' my call ag'in at anodder time."

"Come when de speret moves you," she answered.

It frequently did.

Flora finally resolved that she was not going to waste her life waiting for "a man who didn't care a pin fer her or her chilluns. I'll marry ag'in, but not on Mars Joe's place, ter a fellow always 'round spittin' tobacco juice 'cross de fire, ober pots an' fryin' pans. I don't want ter be cookin' an' waitin' on a man ev'ry day in de week.   I likes my freedom."

Gossiping tongues in the cornfields surmised as to "which girl Robin was courtin' over at Mars Joe's.   Could his brother's wife be housin' an' feedin' him?   Or, would he give his daid Lucy's ring ter a woman not clever 'nough ter keep her lawful husban'? gittin' up a quarrel between two brudders not 'specially fond of each odder?"

Women ready to undertake the task of caring for six motherless children, roundly abused the little ones' father, saying, "What right has Robin ter meddle wid anodder fellow's wife?   Wors' of all, his brother's, who aldo he was tied fas' ter one, an' loving anodder, would have ter hold ter his barg'in till kingdom come, unless a t'under-bolt should 'nihilate Flora."

And Lily, weary of mending and washing for her sister's children, determined that Robin should marry a wife.   Not on any other planta-tion, however ; for, then the new wife couldn't leave her master to assume duties in her hus-band's cabin.

Exasperated at her failure, she confronted the coachman, whose negligence seemed to prevent the "killing of a fatted calf fer a wedden feast fer Robin, who was now makin' a fool o' himself. I's goin' ter tell missus of de disgraceful proceed-in's," she declared one morning suddenly accosting Marlborough. " Womens gits turned out o' de nurs'ry if dey crooks deir finger, but mens does ten times worse an' yit holds tight ter carriage-lines, wid deir head high in air. Here you is day by day wearin' yourself out fer love of Lyddy, leavin' your wife fer Robin, an' he a-lettin' dose mudderless chilluns sleep in de cabin alone night after night."

Marlborough sprang to his feet : " Is dat rascal got a pass to visit my wife at Mars Joe's? I t'ought he was cou'tin' Betty. A yallar free niggar slipped from under my hand, but de nex' man who gits in my path, by God, I'll cut his liver out, if he is my own brudder."

After grooming his master's horses and closing the stable for the night, he hurried to the quarters.

A message, however, to Robin preceded him : " Fer the sake of your sister Lily keep out of de coachman's way, or you may git your throat cut."

Robin, it seems, did not sleep at the cabin with his children, nor yet at Professor Joe's.

At the latter place an exasperated husband waited for him till day-dawn.

A kind of Tennessee family feud now stirred the two estates into a turmoil of confusion. In

7

the spirit of a hunter,—who prizes his game in pro-portion to the difficulty he has had in bagging it,—Robin held to the place he had won at his brother's fireplace, skilfully eluding Marlborough.

Scipio brought the facts before Green Forest's master. "It's my painful duty, sir, ter inform you dat your coachman is pretty nigh finished he brudder ter-night. Dey has been quarr'lin', an' news reachin' me dat dey was wrestlin', I 'rested dem an' was comin' ter you, when your bes' man flirt heself out o' my grip, an' he fly at Robin like a wild cat. In one minute he had him flat of he back pommelin' him right an' left. Bro' John tried to help, but your coachman let fly his fist knockin' Bro' John's front teeth plumb in half. Molbro was jes like a wild beast. From de dark he sing out, 'Come to Lamont's; I'll wait fer you till sun-up.'"

The master, greatly surprised and troubled, hastened to attend to Robin's broken leg. He took from him his pass to visit Professor Joe's.

The following morning at nine o'clock Scipio appeared at the library door holding Marlborough's coat collar. "Here he is, sah! Shall I wait your orders?" He hoped to pull off the jacket of this man who provoked his jealousy.

"You may go. I will see you to-night."

Scraping his feet, he touched his forelock, and turned, while under his breath he murmured, " It's so in dis world, some folks gets de upper hand, even wid deir master. If I had smashed right an' left in de style of last night, foreman as I is, I'd got my punishment; dis man, wid no work to do but drivin' fine horses, is a holdin' his head high in air."

As the library door closed, Marlborough, a truly penitent slave, stepped forward, his face bowed to his breast, his hands tightly clasped.

"O massa," he implored, "do scuse me, sah. I know I is done wrong, but believe me, sah, I couldn't help it. My life is all upside down. Massa, won't you break dat marriage ober at Massa Joe's? I has been back an' tried ter do my best fer Flora, but, my heart ain't dere."

At noon, that day, a stableman espied Marlborough secreted behind one of the carriages, securing a shining object in the inner-lining of his vest. He distinctly heard him say : " I'll use this yet, God helpin' me."

From that time it was an open secret that the coachman carried a bright dagger inside his vest front. Gossip said, too, that no man could look so unhappy if a devil wasn't urging him to an act of violence. "If massa knew 'bout dat knife he'd have him stripped ter de skin." Yet woe

betide the one telling on him! Even Scipio
kept his own counsel.

Marlborough thereafter calmly awaited a favourable time to use his supposed weapon.

"The gods to some are wondrous kind." Affie
declared, "If de devil was in Molbro's heart, de
angels was feedin' him. Why," said she, "he don't
eat 'nough to keep a sparrer. When he come fer
a bite, Lyddy an' de househol' niggars is left de
table, de coffee lost de flavour, an' de biscuits
hard an col'. Massa will miss him if he gits sick
an' dies. An' me! I hates new niggars; dey
takes sech a time to learn decent manners,
neber 'memberin' eben to bring me a pail o'
water."

Knowing the coachman's fondness for his
master's children, Lydia did her best to cheer
him, begging occasionally, "That he'd give the
baby a ride on his shoulder."

"I ain't got no time, I's too pestered. I wish
I was daid, anyhow."

"Bro' Molbro, do don't talk like dat. Is your
heart turned ter stone?"

"Stone, Lyddy! O God! If it was a brickbat I'd laugh an' be happy, dashin' dis away,—"
he tapped his waist-coat,—"but my heart is sore
an' I can't forgit de time when I was de happiest
black man in Siberty County. I'll use this yet!"

he excitedly cried, "even if it's over an open grave."

Catching hold of his coat-sleeve, Lydia pleaded " Will you murder your brother, like Cain ? Oh, Bro' Molbro, give me dat dagger. Is this we coachman who is so good an' kind! Do, Bro' Molbro, cheer up! Don't look troubled. I wouldn't mind all de talk 'bout Flora an' Bro' Robin. Flora is a good 'oman, only you has been neglectin' her ; an' it's my fault. We can neber be more dan friends an' fellow-servants dis side de heav'nly Jerusalem."

Her hand still rested on his sleeve. He clasped it. " Lyddy, my Lyddy, does you believe what massa reads in de Bible 'bout ' God is love?' Oh! if He is,—" then he rushed away, his sentence unfinished, but next his beating heart, was still his unused burnished treasure, awaiting a favourable opportunity for use.

VIII.

Satan's Rope Cut.

" A poor man served by thee shall make thee rich :
A sick man helped by thee shall make thee strong ;
Thou shalt be served thyself by every sense
Of service which thou renderest."

MRS. BROWNING.

DURING Robin's convalescence Lydia was sent frequently to his cabin with dainty food from our table. While there, in a spirit of charity, she tidied his room. Eyeing her wistfully, he begged : " Kind lady, do come ag'in ! de light of your eyes makes my heart leap wid joy. Tell missus eb'ry bite she sends by your hand makes me stronger, Bumbye I'll be at work ag'in."

Waiting outside, Lydia's "white children " watched black youngsters tumble over each other in play. Many were sadly devoid of nether garments ; for boys rarely wore their first pants after the pride of possession had waned. Granny, indeed, had often occasion to unearth these breeches from piles of sand. She replaced them with effective blows of her horny hand, saying, " Is dis de place fer your pantaloons, you imp of a Satan ?"

Lily, the seamstress, with a touch of skill, now enlisted her fellow-worker Nannie into a scheme by which she hoped to put an end to stolen visits over at Professor Joe's.

Nannie was the youngest sister of Marlborough and Robin, and but recently had married Timothy, foreman on Mr. Ben Cay's place, at Barnard's landing. Having been initiated into family secrets, he declared, as his opinion, that only trouble would follow if Lily succeeded ; for the two brothers had, in fact, disagreed from boyhood ; even rending in twain a blanket in a dispute as to who was wrapped in the "Lion's share." Had not the elder brother's marital relations also been interfered with ?

Undaunted, however, by wild-cat grip or fear of a shining dagger, Robin eagerly adopted his sister-in-law Lily's views. Years before he had given Uncle Toby a fat 'possum ! Now he knew his lesson by heart. His face and hands washed in hot soapsuds, round his neck a bright red scarf,— to show his mourning was cast aside,—he donned his " Sunday-go-ter meetin' suit " and beaver hat ; with a limp still in his gait, he hobbled toward a cabin built on the edge of an orange-grove, surrounding his master's mansion.

The February night was laden with the perfume of orange blooms, mingled with odours from honeysuckle and jessamines, their vines clambering over the cabin-door, and trailing and twining about the bell-rope stretched from the nursery to the nurse's cabin.

Brightly shone moon and stars, enhancing the beauty of the scene and tinging the golden fruit with shining lustre.

At Lydia's cabin-door Robin stood with a tremor in his heart, fearing some one else might be inside ;—she was a great favourite on the place.

However, fortune favoured him ; for Lydia sat in front of a blazing pine-fire all alone, mending her children's clothes. In an adjoining shed-room her five youngsters lay sleeping and snoring. Neither cotton nor corn had yet sprouted, therefore Robin found Toby's regulation-topics soon exhausted. But he spoke of the blue and white china glistening on the shelves, taking minute interest in fashion-book prints tacked about the board-walls, the costumes delineated representing hoopskirts covering yards of carpet-space.

" Dear Miss Cummin's," said he, it's a sorry time in a man's cabin, no 'oman settin' in de 'oman's seat. My chilluns is so full of play, dey won't pick a basket of chips ter brown de loaf. I see your boy James has piled up your box wid fat pine-knots."

" My chilluns don't like work no better dan yours. It's we coachman cut de wood."

" Jes like dat rascal! I'll be bound he neber gits a stick fer de chimney-corner ober at Mars Joe's."

" Is you still breakin' massa's law? Ain't you satisfied wid your lame leg ter stay at home? Don't you know Bro' Molbro carries a shinin' dagger in his vest-front. Folks says de bridge ter a man's wife's house is narrow ; if two meets on it, blood may be shed. Take my advice, an' stay at home wid your chilluns."

" My dear an' hon'rable lady," cried Robin, " dat is jes what I is doin', but I must have a mudder fer dem. Seein' you setten dere in a spotless aprin an' black an' w'ite turban, de look in your soft hazel eyes is 'nough ter shake de heart of a lion, let 'lone a man weary livin' by heself. I has brought a bundle of love ter lay at your feet, if you will 'cept of my cou'tship, 'an I'll make you as happy as ever dat brother of mine could."

" Bro' Robin, I's not askin' fer more happiness, I has plenty ter eat an' wear, my house is comf'-table. Massa an' missus treats me like a human,

my ' w'ite chilluns ' dotes on deir mommer, an'
we all rides ter chu'ch in a fine carriage wid de
best pair of horses in Siberty County, not ter
speak of de likeliest coachman.   Bye-de-bye, has
you an' your brother made friends yit?   Night
after night I dreams of a dagger hangin' over my
head, an' I wakes jes as Bro' Molbro pushes it
away, so it won't fall on me."

" Jes like dat coachman ! he's tied to one, an'
is a keepin' watch ober another 'oman les' her
heart gits touched by what folks calls love ; cuttin'
wood here, his lawful weddin' wife is pickin' chips
ter warm his chilluns' toes."

" Judgin' ag'in? Don't you know massa is
ordered de wood cut, caise if de nuss'ry bell rings,
no matter when, I must go.   Missus neber calls
les' some one is ill."

" Most hon'red lady," continued Robin " by
marryin' me you'll shut de mouth of folks what
says you has coaxed Flora's husband ter leave
her."

" I has suffered 'nough already ; don't come here
ter break my heart ! Don't ask me ter marry
you.   I is happier here wid my fatherless chilluns.
Go an' court one of de 'omen's at de quarters.
Dey is more suitable ter your understandin' dan
I is."

" Miss Cummin's, a man can't ask any 'oman ter

be his wife ; he must have a warmin' ter her ; no one has brought my heart ter compose since my poor Lucy died but you, hon'red lady. I'll be better ter you dan ter her, caise now I has been in de 'oman's seat ; I knows de terrification dey has."

Rocking back and forth in her rocker, Lydia replied, " Don't waste your time cout'in' me. Go to your chillun's."

The cabin-door closed behind her visitor. Lydia's trouble found audible voice : " Why are folks talkin' 'bout me ? What has I done ? Ain't dere mercy in heaven ? Must my sin follow me forever ? Is de sighs an' groans of a black person got no power wid de Lord ? Massa reads 'bout golden vials full of saints' tears. I's a slave, not rich 'nough ter buy gold." She lifted her eyes in prayer : " O God, won't you 'cept a glass-bottle full of de truest drops dat ever fell from any one's eyes ? "

She slipped from the chair to her knees, pressing her lips to the leaves of an old Bible that once belonged to her former master, Squire Janeston. " I can't read de Word o' God, but, Jesus, do listen to my cry ! Must de trumphet sound ag'in, Woe ! woe ! woe ! Will de sun turn black an' de moon set like blood ? de burnin' mountain ris' before me ? Lord, thou what talked to Sara in de tent door, speak! tell me what ter do. My heart is as pure as de w'itest w'ite lady, but I hates ter have folks talkin' 'bout my havin' spotted black wings."

She listened, as mysterious, weird words seemed to hiss from behind the blazing logs, " Marry! marry! marry!"

The regulation ghostly three times startled her; she buried her face within the leaves of her Bible; while into low cadence the words died, " Marry! marry! marry!"

Hugging to her bosom the well-worn Bible, she groaned, "O, dear Jesus, is dat what you wants me ter do?"

The following day mother noticed a strange look of trouble on her nurse's face. But not even to Marlborough did Lydia tell of her heavenly visitant.

Robin, the ensuing night, shut his cabin door, leaving his motherless children in front of the fire, huddled on the floor, sound asleep. He picked his way to Lydia's chimney, and peered through a crevice from the outside, to make sure that no visitor was within.

He entered and earnestly renewed his court-ship; but Lydia replied; " I has lost faith in men's folks, Bro' Robin. I has had one good husband, but it's sech men what gets drownded. No 'count folks lives on an' on, fussin' 'bout trifles, like de quality of gol' rings, talkin' of wings tipped wid de stain of sin. I knows one t'ing, if it wa'n't fer you mens-folks' talk, we 'omens' plumes would be w'ite like snow. You mens is de most on you black as crows wid your guilt. No wonderment is made ober your foul fedders, but jes let a dove show a dark fedder an' howls an' hisses sounds on eb'ry side. If you crows would stay in de cornfield, where you belongs certain sure doves wouldn't leave deir dove-cote ter hunt fer you."

Saturday night Flora sat singing to her young baby, wondering if Marlborough would spend Sunday with her. She had heard old women comment on the youngster's strong resemblance to its Uncle Robin, but, happily, she was once more on fairly good terms with her lawful husband, and so she wisely kept her tongue. She listened anxiously for well-known footsteps.

At cock-crow she was roused from her fruitless wait. Indeed, he who should have been by her side was fulfilling a duty he felt due to his kind master. For weeks Marlborough had suspected that the orange trees about Lydia's cabin were being robbed. Accordingly, he secreted himself in readiness to spring upon the thief.

Three taps on Lydia's door startled him. To

a negro three taps means a visit with a precon-
ceived purpose.

From his hiding-place he sprang, and the next
moment he was on the ground struggling with a
man in his firm grip.

"What business has you a tappin' at dis dooe?
Did I bring wood ter warm you, you rascal? I'll
cut your liver out"—throwing himself over
Robin, who screamed lustily, "Sis Liddy, Sis
Liddy, come quick, a dagger is cuttin' my throat."
His voice grew more and more suppressed, with
gurgling sounds.

Lydia rushed to the rescue, and wound her
arms about Marlborough's neck, without casting
aside the stocking in which her hand was encased.
Consequently, the needle buried itself in his neck
and broke uncomfortably near his jugular vein.
"Bro' Molbro!" she cried, "What are you doin',
stabbin' your own brother at my very dooe! O
God, ain't I suffered 'nough yit?"

Pointing to the negro quarters, Marlborough
said, "Go, sah, where you belong! You is not
worthy ter sweep de trash from dese steps, let
'lone goin' inside ter set beside de fire-place.
Let me catch you here ag'in an' I'll pound your
bones ter powder."

Resistance was worse than vain; so, with
crushed beaver and soiled Sunday-clothes, Robin,

the lover, walked away, not one whit undecided, however, as to his future efforts.

In the cabin Lydia essayed to withdraw the needle-point. But she was caught in a warm embrace, which instinctively she returned, their lips meeting in an ecstasy of feeling: "My Lyddy, my heart's love, before heaven you are my wife; come, be mine! God knows how I loves you!"

She tore herself away, then leaned upon the mantel-shelf, moaning, "It's all my fault, it's a curse followin' me. Why did I listen ter that rascal wid his talk 'bout silk frocks an' freedom? Bro' Molbro, we might have married, but it's too late now. Dey calls me a slave. Yes, I am a slave, but my slave-wings must be kept pure an' w'ite."

"Dey is pure an w'ite, my Lyddy. Jacob waited fer Rachel seven years; my seven is turned de eight, an' you ain't yit my wife. Massa hates a lie. Don't I lie eb'ry time I goes ter Mars Joe's? Come, Lyddy, let's go ter massa and missus, an' once more beg dem ter untie de knot what's chained me ter Flora. Den you'll be my wife, won't you? I can't live dis way; my heart will break."

"It's too late; it's too late, Bro' Molbro, it's me done dis deed o' murder. Give me de dagger;

let me drag from my own heart what God he-self put dere. I ain't ashamed ter tell you how much I used ter love you. But it's too late! Go, go! Be good ter Flora, an' try ter forgit all de wrong I has done you."

"If I could forgit, Liddy; but I can't. I has neber wanted freedom, yet now I must be free ter make money ter buy my Lyddy. If dis ain't possible, will you run away wid me? Folks say dere is an underground way, an' at de odder end w'ite ladies feeds us wid deir own hands. Come, will you go dis very night? Look, it's not too late, we could be safe before daybreak. Our mar-riage was 'ranged in heaven. Let's have it set-tled on earth. Come, git ready, Lyddy, we will start at once."

"Don't talk so fas', Bro' Molbro. No matter where you goes, Flora is your wife; fer Mars C. C. said, 'before God I pronounces you man an' wife.'"

"If w'ite folks breaks up niggar marriages, that don't count. Why can't we do de same?" pro-tested Marlborough.

"Has you t'ought 'bout leavin' your master an' my w'ite chilluns? Dey would weep deir eyes out fer deir mommer. I'd be mis'rable 'way from dem, an' Mars C. C. would blot my name from de chu'ch books."

"Lyddy, I loves my massa an' all his fam'ly, but as I can't marry you here, we must go where I can. Be quick, tie up your clothes in a bundle; come, I'll help."

Three times the bell over his head clanged, like a note from heaven. Quick as a flash Lydia darted out the door, knowing that some one she loved was ill.

Marlborough then seated himself in the rocking chair, and covered his face with his hands; he was quivering with excitement. Seemingly oblivious to his companion's absence, he murmured: "It's so, Lyddy, I couldn't live 'way from we good w'ite folks. Satan has his rope 'round my neck."

Snatching Lydia's Bible from the mantel-shelf, he pressed his lips upon its cover: "I'll cut dat debil's cord, an' wait. Caise massa says, 'God is love.'"

On his knees he sank, with his black hands folded across his breast, as if to retain his treasure more securely.

The ensuing night the usual hush and quiet crept over the plantation. Now and then a sentinel gander gave a signal to let his flock know that he was on duty. The air was cold, and Lydia drew her chair close beside the dying embers. She nodded, from loss of sleep.

8

"Marry! Marry! Marry!" again whizzed through the chimney-jamb, startling her from her dreams.

Though clever herself in invoking aid from supernatural spirits when needed for her "w'ite chilluns," she, nevertheless, was now under the domination of an angel voice. So, fearing to sit in the presence of an heavenly visitant, she knelt, reaching for her Bible, her safeguard in time of anxiety. "O Lord, tell me de name? Is it Bro' Molbro? Show me dy will, O God! Speak so I kin hear."

The feeble flame flared, as if blown upon: "Ro-ro-bin! Ro-ro-bin! Ro-ro-bin!"

"Great God! Hast thou oberlooked de sharp dagger what Bro' Molbro carries? Must I marry Bro' Robin?"

Lydia was roused at early dawn from her troubled sleep by the sound of partridges in the fields beyond her cabin. One after another they whistled to their mates "Ro-ro-bin! Ro-ro-bin! Ro-ro-bin!"

Wiping her face with a wet rag, she hurried to the nursery, to get out of reach of three words, that seemed urging her on to her doom.

Before her arrival, however, Caroline, Marlborough's mother, had snugly ensconced herself in front of a blazing fire, kindled for the children to dress by. Contented, she was testing roasted yams, that had been covered the preceding night beneath red-hot oak ashes, to be ready for hungry young mouths.

Our assistant nurse, nick-named Old Soul, was a peaceable creature, not troubling herself, it appeared, even about the broil between her two sons.

Eccentric in many ways, she never wore shoes, and clicked her bare heels together in walking. Her manner of rousing us from sleep was unheard of, and mother would have shuddered to have seen her in early morning lift our bed-covers at the foot of the bed, grasp our pink feet, then, one after another, pull the toes until they gave a click, as if the muscles had stretched beyond their limit. Were this not sufficient to send us kicking and howling out of bed, she treated our fingers to the same.

Old Soul gloried in listening to fairy tales concocted by Lydia. Lydia's most startling experience, however, was not told until years after its occurrence.

Her narrations of Bro' Wolf and Bro' Rabbit, we never forgot. And I vividly recall the excitement of listening to her tales. With fiery flashing insects in our handkerchiefs we watched, and waited, hoping and expecting they would momentarily expand into live and radiant fairies, ready to gratify our every wish. This, we were assured by our nurse, would be the case if we sat "as still as mice."

The beauty of our lawns of the summer evenings was of incomparable charm, innumerable fireflies, or "lightning-bugs," as vulgarly termed, flitting fantastically from side to side.

IX.

A Spanish Trading=Port.

" And more true joy Marcellus exiled feels
Than Cæsar with a senate at his heels."

POPE.

AS history records, St. Augustine, Florida, was at one time a busy Spanish trading-port, as well as in Colonial days a landing-place for native Africans. Later, it also became a famous negro mart. Even now the remains of a fort continue to attract visitors that journey south, to winter, under tropical suns, and among orange-groves with perfume-laden sea-air. But of the many visitors attracted there yearly, few, I fancy, give a thought to the aborigines that were driven from their land of flowers to ice-bound regions. Mrs. Harriet Beecher Stowe—whose book, "Uncle Tom's Cabin," thrilled the universe, I confess—had her winter home in this part of the south, where both good and bad masters brought their slaves to be sold.

About ten years ago, fire, happily, destroyed

the old shed and block (remnants of barbarity), where thousands of human beings were sold like cattle or sheep.   Here, too, were kept a pack of blood-hounds, ready to scent fugitive slaves, who dared attempt to escape from a cruel owner. Strangely enough, the auctioneer was always a northern man.

Caesar, Machiah, and hundreds of other slaves were bought here and transferred to Green Forest. Marlborough's master, on one occasion, occupied himself before the auction by noting the good points of those to be sold.   A likely lad, industriously whittling a white-oak strip, attracted him.

Accosting him, he said, " My boy, what are you making ? "

" A bow, ah ! "

" A bow !   Surely, at your age, you don't play with bow and arrows, do you ? "

" I kin stretch a bow as good as de best of dem —kin bring down a turkey or steer when we comes 'cross one."

" Is that right ? would you kill a steer that did not belong to you."

" You see, boss," he replied, " Pow-wow swears de cows in de oak-lands an' de boars in de cane-break ain't nobody's ; so, by occasion, we kills a fat fellow."

" Who is Pow-wow ? "

"Dat Injin yonder," pointing to a Cherokee warrior, partly robed and partly plumed, who was leaning against a post of the auction-shed, looking on merely as a matter of curiosity; or, perhaps, hoping to sell Indian wares.

"What's your name, my boy?"

"Abel, sah."

"Where is your father?"

"Never had none."

"There you are mistaken, Abel; everybody must have had a father."

"I reckon Pow-wow is my pa."

"No, indeed; you are too black, and your hair too kinky to be the son of a red Indian. Is that your mother over there nursing her baby?"

"I don't 'member my mudder, 'cept dat she lick me one night."

"How long is it since you've seen her?"

"Nigh on ter eighty moons."

"Impossible! You are not more than sixteen years old now."

"Boss says I's twenty."

"Who is the boss?"

"Dat man wid de brass buttons; you'll see him mount de block presently."

"So, you have been sold here before?"

"No, sah! I come one day wid Pow-wow, an' de boss tell him to bring me ter-day. He say some buckra' man would buy me. Massa, won't you bid fer me? I likes you; caise you talks good."

"Then you have been living with Pow-wow? Are you just from the wigwam?

"It's three moons since I fus quit de Injins. Old man Thorne pick up a stick ter make me go an' hoe he turnip patch; but I tell him last week I wouldn't stay dere; I likes Floridy de best. We has gumbo an' oranges; turkey is plenty, too."

"Where is Thorne?"

"You see dat man standin' 'longside a critter wid a calico colt? Dat's he."

A tall scrawny pine-land cracker busily adjusted the girth of his saddle. He covertly watched my father questioning Abel, wondering, doubtless, what they could find to talk about.

"Tell me your mother's name, Abel."

"Miss call um cook."

"You had a missis, then! What was her name? Was it Thorne's wife?"

"She ain't no missis; she 's poor cracker. She ain't no better dan me. I sits 'longside Becky at table; she's de oldest gal of de fam'ly, an' kin skin a sheep as good as de Injins. She beats her baby jes like it was stone."

"How did you happen to leave your mother

when so young? Can't you recall her name? Did your master sell you?"

"I 'members one night I was tired sleepin', so I was goin' in de dark ter de quiltin' an' somebody give me a long stick o' candy. We trotted on horseback, an' when I wake up I was sleepin' in de bed wid lots of w'ite chilluns. I didn't have no breeches, so dey gib me one of de w'ite boy's. We chilluns play in de log-house, an' when I cry ter go out, de old w'ite 'oman hol' me. She say it ware too hot; I better stay 'long side de fire."

"Did you live there long?" asked my father, smiling at this incoherent speech.

"I's done forgot, sah. We ride on horseback ag'in, an' when I wake up Pow-wow squaw was feedin' me wid gumbo and oranges."

"Have you been ever since with Pow-wow and his children?"

"I's all de chilluns dey's got."

"Why did Pow-wow want to sell you?"

"Dat old cracker Thorne tried ter fight wid Pow-wow 'bout me; den Wunda say dey better sell me an' share de money."

"Is Wunda your squaw-mother?"

"She's good to me. I likes her; she cooks fine gumbo. Massa, does you have any gumbo turkey? Becky's husband say dis mornin' dat if

I tell folks I's been libin wid de Injins, some fine night he'll tie me ter a tree head down, an' he'll cut out my tongue an' roast it in de fire. I's 'fraid o' fire. Massa, don't tell folks what I tell you. I's gettin' scared."

"You are safe, Abel, but why are you so afraid of fire?"

"I fall in de fire once an' burn my arm w'ite."

"You did! I must see that scar; I won't buy you if you are unable to work."

Having arranged his saddle, Thorne sneaked around to where Abel stood behind a house; he removed his jacket, while father examined the white scar on his left arm.

With suspicious eyes Pow-wow was restless, his feathers waving in the sea-breeze.

Recourse to the law, in order to stop the sale of Abel, would have required time, giving Pow-wow another opportunity to secrete his foster-son in the dense canebrakes of Florida. Father deemed it important to take the boy Abel to Siberty County as soon as possible.

The auctioneer, therefore, agreed to give a deed of sale at once, swearing that he himself had bought the boy from Phil Hertz, down at Tampa Bay.

At the homestead, when Marlborough reined in his horses, it was dark. "Have your supper

with the boy Abel," his master said, and be at
the gate by eight o'clock with fresh horses. I
must drive to Mr. Winn's plantation."

We gathered about father, begging he would
tell us how many Indian squaws, with their pap-
pooses, he had seen in Florida. But he kissed
us good-night, with the words, "Be good children ; to-morrow after breakfast you shall hear a
real true Indian story."

The rumbling of carriage-wheels aroused Mr.
Winn, who was dozing beside his library fire.
Opening the door himself, he greeted his visitor :

"Good evening, neighbour. Come in and have
a cigar. I've just opened a fresh box of the best
Havanas."

"Thank you, not now; I am in a hurry. I
hear your cook is very ill."

"She is, faithful old soul; she will hardly last
another twenty-four hours. I was with her a
good part of last night. But she's growing
weaker, day and night calling for her boy John.
Every time the door opens she imagines it's he."

"Let's go to her at once. Do you think she'll
recognise me ?"

"I can't say. An hour ago her mind was still
wandering. She talked incessantly of her lost
son, eaten by a big black bear. You know,
friend Janes, I have a feeling that that fellow was

never eaten. I am inclined to join in the superstition that has taken hold of the negroes in the
quarters, that John will some day come back, for
his mother seems clearly to see him."

Talking earnestly, the two planters reached the
cabin. Marlborough and Abel followed in the
rear.

An aged granny sat in the room nodding by
the bed of a dying woman, whose only child
Amy, soon to be motherless, lay sound asleep on
the floor.

Mr. Winn spoke. Then his visitor greeted the
sufferer: "Are you feeling better to-night, old
woman? I hope you are as happy as you used
to be in Greenville some years ago."

"T'ank you, massa. I feels pow'ful weak."

"Do you know me?"

"Yes, sah, I knows you; it's Mars Janes. You
kill dat big black bear what eat my boy John.
Is you got de skin on your floor yit, sah?"

"Feede, Feede, listen! Suppose I told you
no black bear ever touched your son, would you
believe me?"

At the name "Feede," Abel, who stood in
front of the fire, sprang to the bedside.

"Ma," he cried, "is dat you?" Then he
peered into her half-closed eyes.

Weak and exhausted, Feede continued:

"Massa, does you t'ink when I gits ter heaven I'll
find John dere? Kin de Lord resurrect him from
the maw of de bear? If I could only see my
boy once more! Amy! push up the fire, ma's
gittin' cold."

"Ma! ma!" continued Abel, "here's your
John! Here I is, ma! No bear eat me! Don't
you know me? I ain't name Abel; I's name
John. Don't you 'member you spanked me an'
kivered me head an' ears when you was a-going'
ter de quiltin'?"—throwing his arms round her
neck.

Startled, Feede returned the embrace. "Bless
de Lord! I's find my boy." Her glazed eyes
fastened upon his face. "Pull up your sleeve,
John; let ma see de w'ite scar."

"Mars Janes," she cried, "here sure 'nough's
my John! Did you kill de bear?" She gasped
a few times, then fell back upon her pillow;—her
fingers patted the coverlid.

"Lie down, John, lie down, let ma kiver you
up. Ma's goin' cross de riber, but ma 'll be back
bumbye."

By the influence of a hidden sense, that needed
but a trifle to kindle into life a dead memory,
Abel picked up the lost thread that bound him
to the past: a familiar but forgotten name
brought all to mind.

After Feede's funeral, father bought Amy.
When packing her mother's effects, she found a
pair of little pants, securely bound up with a bright
patchwork quilt that Dean's cook had given
Feede. The latter had never been used; for,
with negro superstition, no one would lie beneath
a covering that had cost a mother so much sorrow.

We were to hear a real Indian story before
breakfast, but Lydia forestalled her master.
Shaking each child excitedly, she said, "Jump up,
chilluns, de heavens is weepin' fer joy! de ground
is w'ite wid angels' tears! Bro' Molbro say he
couldn't sleep las' night fer singin' hallalujah!
Dat old bear from Bulltown swamp galloped to
Floridy an' puked de boy John plumb 'fore a
Injin's' wigwam; he was pleased wid de mudderless child; so de squaw feed him wid gumbo
soup an' oranges. Would you believe it, chilluns,
he is growd ter be a big man? It's de same fellow what eat supper in de kitchin las' night.
Nobody know'd him. Down in Floridy de Injin
warrior mus' a liked massa's talk, caise he give
him John ter bring ter his mudder, Feede. When
she seed de w'ite scar, she pulled up de quilt
what Dean's cook give her an' she patted John's
head: 'Lie down, John, let ma kiver you up,
I's goin' ober de riber Jordan, but ma's sperit
will come bumbye an' keep comp'ny wid you.'

Den old Feede dropped back daid. Be quick, chilluns, and dress;·le's go an' fill a bottle wid de angels' tears, fer it looks like a big fedder bed from de golden city is turned loose in de wind."

Having never before seen a fall of snow, our nurse's original explanation of a snow-storm suited our excitable young minds.

In the confusion of dressing, three loud knocks at the adjoining window sent us, one and all, pell-mell into Lydia's arms, with soap, sponge, shoes, stockings, frocks, comb, and brush.

" Massa," a voice called, " old Jerry is daid, sah ; stiff as a board."

The horse Jerry was a great favourite with the children, letting them clamber on his broad old back. He was one of a pair bought in Maine. Father surmised that Jerry had sniffed the keen cold air, and, in his efforts to get out and into it, he had, by his own force, throttled himself. All the horses were now turned out. Tom, Jerry's mate, at once laid himself down, rolling in the snow with evident pleasure. The southern bred animals, however, sought the warm stable.

Exemplifying the force of early education, we, as all southern children, never thought of the dark side of slavery; we lived regardless of its evil consequences. Similarly, also, knitters

in the Place de la Concorde, who dropped a stitch
to tally with human heads falling into the basket,
proved that they were inured to the spectacle,
apparently seeing only the bright and happy side
of life.

X.

Marlborough and his Brute Friend.

" Tears, sighs, prayers fail, but true love lasteth ever."
                                    ROBERT JONES.

FEBRUARY'S blooms, beaten about by March winds, lay on the ground, mouldering. Overhead, festoons of grey moss hung like a funeral shroud. As an earnest of the future, the limbs from which this trailing moss swayed, showed here and there the lifegiving power of spring. Peach and plum trees were already weighted with a wealth of embryo fruit, rounded and enlarged each day. Innumerable pear-shaped figs protruded from dry branches; for fig trees show no gay blooms as forerunners of a frugal crop.

Labourers were busy in corn and cotton fields, their hoes glistening with constant friction against mother-earth. The brisker the work, the merrier the glee, on all southern estates.

Green Forest was no exception. Robin's voice, clear and loud, indicated a new joy had

9

come to supplant his dead memory. His happiness struck a vibrating cord in the throats of field-lark and thrush; the woods were resonant with song.

This reinvigoration of flowers and birds failed, however, to reinspire our nurse's songs: they sounded like funeral dirges. Old April Fool even forgot to play his pranks with the children.

One day my mother asked Lydia why she had a sad countenance? "Are you ill?"

"T'ank you, ma'am, I's all right, only tryin' ter do my duty. Missus, may I marry Bro' Robin?" Her voice indicated that she half-wished the permission would be withheld.

"I have no objection, if you think you will be happier as his wife. You already have a houseful of children, and it seems to me that, with Robin's six, you will have much care."

"It's so, ma'am, but ain't dere times when one must do deir best ter fulfil de will o' God?"

"Yes. If you look upon it as God's will, it's all right. Has Marlborough taught you to believe all marriages are made in heaven? Poor fellow, he will lose his faith in this instance."

"Bro' Molbro don't know it, ma'am, an' it's fer dat I don't want ter be married in de chu'ch. Won't massa ask Mars C. C. to 'form de ceremony in de nuss'ry?"

" You may be married in the parlour or dining-
room if you wish."

" De nuss'ry is de sweetest place in de world,
ma'am. I want my w'ite chilluns round about.
Please don't give me a wedden' feast."

No one talked about the approaching marriage,
arranged by preternatural power. An account of
the spiritual influence reached Flora, awing her
into silence.

With heavy heart Affie beat a cake light, groan-
ing over the fact that, morning by morning, Marlborough's coffee was weakened with briny drops.
Stunned as he had been by the interposition of
heaven in ringing the bell overhead when he was
following Satan's lead, he, nevertheless, not by a
single word, let it be known that he was aware of
his brother's good fortune.

One Saturday afternoon, April twentieth, Dr.
C. C. drove to Green Forest to spend the night.
Sunday he was due to preach at Pleasant Grove
Church. About eight o'clock in the evening, Old
Soul, Lily, Juno, James and Georgia,—Nanny
and Jack, with two broken front teeth,—stood
in line against the nursery wall.

The door opened, and the venerable Dr. C. C.
entered, leaning upon the arm of Green Forest's
master, who was holding in his hand a well-worn
Bible, brought from England many years before.

In the rear followed the mistress, her group of children visibly excited and looking behind. Then came a woman neatly dressed in a blue calico-print, with tucked cambric apron and snow-white bandanna. Beside her walked a man as black as ebony.

A short prayer, a scripture lesson, and the clergyman said: "In the name of the Lord I pronounce you husband and wife. What God hath joined together let not man put asunder. Amen!"

In his usual happy way, he then shook hands, wishing Lydia and Robin joy in their new relationship. The master and mistress did the same. From one to another the children handed silver baskets filled with slices of cake.

Lydia, kissing their dainty hands, whispered, "Call mommer when you's sleepy."

"Mamma says Old Soul and Lily can put us to bed to-night," piped up Letha.

"No dey won't, needer. I'll not neglect my w'ite chilluns fer anybody."

Marlborough fully understood the purport of this clerical visit; it extinguished his last ray of hope. Into a trough he dashed a measure of corn and bundle of fodder, then he haltered the parson's tired old mare in front of it, scarcely removing from its ill-kept coat the dust of travel.

Long past his hours of work the heartsick man groomed old Bolivar, first with curry-comb, then with brush. The hide of the worn-out animal, unaccustomed to such attention, was sore rather than refreshed, and he switched his tail and stamped, first one foot then the other, trying, in brute language, to indicate that he had enough.

"Be still, Bolivar! Ain't you learned to obey yit? All my life I has been obliged ter do what I was told ter do; be still, old fellow!" He leaned forward and whispered into his furry ear, "Does you hear a sledge-hammer poundin' heavy blows on my heart? Yit I must keep still w'ile dat rascal calls my Lyddy his wife." To suppress his anger, he gritted his teeth. "Massa's been good ter you an' me, ain't he, old horse? It's only dat what keeps me from followin' Cain. I couldn't live an' hear my name called as massa called it one morning in de library." He clasped his arms round the muscular neck of the dumb creature.

"Yes, Bolivar, you an' me is in bondage. Eat your corn, old fellow, wid a t'ankful heart, caise you ain't got no mind ter be cut up as I is. My mouth is bitter. Yonder, folks is eatin' sweet cake. I can't help myself caise I's a slave.

He pressed his hand over his breast, where lay his alleged dagger, then back on the hot side of

the old horse he leaned.   Many years before, he
had driven Bolivar from Riseburg, with a young
woman beside him, on the carriage front.

"If what massa says is true dat ' God is love,'
O Lord, do let me keep dis till I kin win my
Lyddy, my angel wid snow-w'ite wings."

With the tenderness of a woman he caressed
his hidden treasure, that some day was to fulfil
its mission, even over an open grave.

XI.

Lot Number Four.

"The golden circlet of life's work well done
Set with the shining pearl of perfect rest."

IN May, as usual, we again left the plantation for our summer residence. Robin visited his wife twice a week, bringing with him a bag of children's clothes to be washed : his wife excelled as a laundress.

During that summer, the household servants evinced much uneasiness, because three mornings in succession, Fido, the family pet, had been seen dragging his left-hind leg.

Another uncanny omen startled them when two cranes, which seldom come near human habitations, settled upon the balustrade, beside the mistress' bedchamber.

Lydia shouted at them. Whereupon one flew away, soon followed by the other.

Months passed, but nothing happened to verify the evil omens.

When hot, sultry days gave place to a glorious

Indian summer, with its clear, crispy-cool mornings, we rejoiced. For, after the second frost, it was safe to return to the home in the oaklands which we loved.

October had now but one day before it would drop from the year's calendar, and, as its last sun was sinking in the west, a baby-boy arrived.

The natal song was hardly sung, and night was slowly throwing about the earth its sombre garment, when the angel of death folded his wings above the mother's couch. Calling Chim, the eldest-born, she committed the cradled infant to her care, saying: " When we are gone, I know you will be a mother and father to your sisters and brothers." Turning to Lydia, she whispered: " Take good care of my little baby boy.'

The news of the mistress' death, transmitted to Green Forest, caused profound consternation and grief. Nearly all our slaves came to the funeral, accompanied by others from adjoining estates. The spacious summer residence was crowded with friends, the coloured people standing about the steps and gate. As the cortège moved toward Midway Cemetery, with hundreds following, there broke forth a cry of sorrow. Like a dead march muffled in sound, they moaned, " We dear good misses is daid," their words followed by sobs and low cries of anguish.

Beside the hearse a small white dog ran, saliva dropping from the tip of his tongue. The negroes declared he was weeping. The loving wife, mother, and mistress was laid beneath an ancient live-oak, burdened with grey moss.

Her little dog Fido soon pined and died; and when the time came to bury it, Lydia and her "w'ite chilluns" stood in mute grief, while Marlborough dug for it a grave beside the myrtle bush. There he had heard the death-knell of his brightest hopes—Marmaduke pleading with the one woman he loved.

Nanny, the waitress, also had presented her husband with a fine healthy black baby, that they called Lucy Ann, after its dead aunt.

Touched by the wails of the little white orphan, Nanny timidly besought her master to allow her to nourish the child, saying, " My Lucy is strong an' well, she kin drink milk."

With a grief that was almost breaking his heart, her master assented: " God bless you! do your best and you will be rewarded."

Tim Cay often declared that his wife loved the boy better than the girl. For if they both cried, the foster-mother comforted the one, but allowed Lucy Ann to expend her best efforts in dilating her lungs.

I again copy a few words from the old planta-

tion diary; inasmuch as they prove the relationship that existed between at least one master and
his slaves.

January 13th.

This is Chim's birthday, and I realise that her loving
companionship has helped me to bear the desolation of
my life.   Much comfort comes, too, from my negroes,
who, while at work in the fields, do their utmost to cheer
me, saying, "Massa, we is broken-hearted, but de will of
de Lord mus' be done. Don't fret, sah, we people is
a-doin' all we kin fer you an' missus' chilluns."

A few golden crocuses peeped above the soggy
earth, smiling, as it were, over the departure of
winter's sharp frosts. On the air came faint
odours, intimating that somewhere, in sheltered
corners, violets bloomed.

A crimson flush burned upon the master's
cheek, and he removed to Greenville for change.
It was beautiful there then! Spring buds had
burst into blossom; birds, happily mated, built
their nests in tree-tops, carolling their love-songs.
But again an angel stopped in his flight, saying:
"Enter ye into the courts above." The gate of
the celestial city, thus once more opened, that two
loving hearts might be reunited. Another wail
of mourning resounded in that pine-land village.

Marlborough believed more than ever that marriages were recorded in heaven. Beside the corpse

Lydia and he seemed to hear music sounding, angels wafting their white robes, crying, " De bridegroom comes on de wing of de mornin', castin' crowns at de feet o' de Lord."

" Bro' Molbro," she said, "I seed missus last night comin' wid outspread wings, holdin' a gold-en-haired boy by de han', that died when my James was a baby; den all de choir o' angels bowed deir heads fer when massa an' missus met it was too sacred fer dem to look at. ' Dwell from hence in my fadder's house where is many mansions.' Ain't dat de word, Bro' Molbro ?"

" Yes, my Lyddy; dere is a house not made wid hands fer you an' fer me, too, when we is dun wid de tribulations o' dis world; you'll have a crown o' gol' wid Lyddy writ on it, so soap an' water can't wash it out. Will you be my wife dere?" he asked, pleadingly.

Her tears choked her reply into inaudible sound.

To this day, rich and poor recall with pleasure the merry voice and sweet speech of Green Forest's master. And for years after his death, his loving slaves greeted us with affectionate assurances, as, " We poor orphan chilluns! De Lord bless we good massa's chilluns."

Father's estate, according to law, had to be assessed and divided; for he left no will. Had he been a resident of Great Britain, Fleming would have come into possession of the landed property, with the greater part of his father's money.

Happily, each of us shared equally our parent's property.

Neither whites nor blacks cared to express preferment as to owner or owned ; although on the day of the division one or two old women dared to whisper, " I's praying I may fall ter you, honey," or " you," as fancy dictated.

Letha confided to me that she cared little whom she drew, except that list with Scipio at its head. " He's too grand and overpowering. I'd never know how to talk to him."

In dollars and cents, however, he was the most valuable of the lot.   Later, Letha's involuntary expression of dismay, told that her fears were re-alized. In my hand was slip number four, headed with Lydia's name and the names of her family.

I did not wait to run down the column, but, delighted, darted out the front door, to where the plantation people were congregated.

" Mommer, you are mine ! " I cried.

In an instant she clasped me to her bosom, my arms wound round her neck.   Other slaves kissed my hands, and even my feet, saying, " We missy ; we Miss Dodo ? "

What similar scenes were enacting round and about never occurred to me to note. The world, recently shrouded in gloom, was now bright. For she who loved our father and mother would never leave me. No picture of happiness was ever painted with brighter colours. Neither the fear of death nor a thought of Lydia's freedom ever intruded to rob that hour of its sweet happiness; she belonged to me, and would be always near to brush away my tears.

Lydia went from one to another, comforting them, saying: " Never mind, mommer will come to see you," seeming to think our household was at once to be broken up.

Hetty, clinging to the baby, called him her "little massa."

" Wid her last breath, missus told me to take care o' him, an' nobody shall part us. Shall dey, sonny?" And Lydia hugged and kissed the crowing child.

Juno, a "deed of gift" to me years before, was not included in the appraisement.

Marlborough fell to the lot of Chim, thereby greatly delighting her, as he had been nearer to his master than any other slave on the place.

Fleming drew Lily, the seamstress.

But time passed, and Letha and Dodo—myself—soon entered a college for young ladies.

XII.

Juno's Wedding Festivities.

"When you get married I'll wait on you."

IN southern climates girls develop rapidly, assuming womanly duties when they should still be in short frocks. While yet scarcely more than a child, Letha, accordingly, married her cousin, a captain in the regular army. He had served his country in Mexico.

One year after, old Jacob mounted his pony and delivered invitations to neighbours for the marriage of Dodo, Lydia's mistress, to a tall, handsome youth, hardly past his teens.

Rumor said that Revilo Bee, years before, had vowed that he would wed Dodo, then a ten-year-old girl weeping over her mother's bier.

Believing that marriages were recorded in heaven, Marlborough and Lydia watched with interest the first intimation of love-making that Revilo manifested when he visited Green Forest or Greenville.

In time, then, under the roof of the old homestead, "two lives with but a single thought"
were united, and on that winter wedding-day
mocking-birds trilled their richest notes in lieu
of a wedding-march.

Juno stood at the steps, the envy of all her associates, while hundreds of blacks awaited the
moment to shower rice upon the pathway of the
newly-wedded pair.

Juno's attire, as well as her wardrobe, had been
arranged with great care. For, she declared, the
bride would be adjudged in her new home by the
appearance of her maid. For the journey she
wore a print frock, with blue drawn-cambric
bonnet lined with pink, her face merry with delight, in spite of the fact that she was soon to be
separated from her former girl-associates.

Her mother's farewell words rang in her
ears:

"Be a good gal. Don't let your young massa
have cause ter scold you. Be sure you takes care
of your nice frocks an' missus' wedden clothes."

Later, at Swansea, Lydia took her position as
chief servant; often, indeed, giving advice as to
how matters should be conducted. I continued
to be one of her "w'ite chilluns," subject to her
imperative commands. For, as is well-known,
southern mammies, with all their tender-hearted-

ness, were often exacting. In truth, more than one young mistress has wept tears of bitterness rather than wound the feelings of a dear old woman that had cuddled her lovingly when childish griefs seemed insupportable.

Maids in all lands are wont to imitate their mistresses. It was not long, therefore, before Juno found her susceptible heart touched. Mastering her naturally timid nature, she informed me one morning that she wished to make a confession.

"Well!" I said, "what have you broken to-day? All my parlour ornaments will be destroyed by your carelessness. I warn you to be careful of our lovely Dresden vases."

Giving a short cough, she replied, "I wants fer tell you,"—then another cough came to her aid.

"You would tell me that you were looking out the window while dusting the mantel, and so did not mean to break anything?"

"Missy, I's sure I ain't broke de fus t'ing. I want's fer tell you dat Dick,"—her cough again interrupted her speech.

"Oh, it's Dick, then, that has been doing damage. I suppose he has ridden my horse Beulah lame, when he has orders never to mount her.

"Don't scold poor Dick, missy, he neber gits on Beulah. I knows, caise we walks ter de spring, de mare a-pullin' de line, a-nibblin' young grass."

"If what Dick has done is a pure accident," "I will have to forgive him, for he seems to be a good sort of fellow."

"He's mighty good an' kind, ma'am. We was goin' ter water de pony yisterday when Dick plant he foot down, an' say: 'Juno, I can't sleep; dis t'ing must be 'cided one way or todder.'" She stuck her forefinger between her pearly white teeth, then bent her head to one side.—"What would you say, missy, if you was me?"

"Juno, have you lost your wits? "What are you talking about? Lace my boots, and let me finish dressing."

"Daniel is a-begging me too, ma'am;" she resumed, after a brief pause, "fer say de same t'ing."

Lydia, her mother, fortunately entered the room.

"What trouble is this brewing, Lydia, I said. Juno is trying to confess some complication with both Daniel and Dick. Do you know of it?"

"Shoh! Shoh! Silly gal, is you fread o' your good missy? Don't make a fool o' yourself. Say square an' plain dat dese fellows has cou't you an' dat you wants ter marry one of dem."

10

"It's the boys' hearts, then, Juno, that you've been breaking, instead of china? I suppose they are crushed into atoms."

"It's so, ma'am! Dey say deir hearts is all gone ter pieces, an' nobody kin mend dem but me. If you was me which would you 'cide on?"

"Indeed, this is a curious state of affairs! You want your husband chosen for you, from among so many good-looking fellows! Suppose the one that I select is not the one recorded in heaven! You'd be tearing each other's wool, or fretting as poor Marlborough did. Some one then would write in a book that darkie girls are not allowed to choose their own husbands, and would thus excite the sympathy of the whole world. I can help you a little. Which do you think is the handsomest, Dick or Daniel?"

"Dick is heap handsomer dan Daniel! he's six foot! Daniel's head ain't no higher dan mine."

"He is older and perhaps a better man," I ventured.

"Law, ma'am, Dick neber tells me a lie. Daniel is all de time foolin'. He promise me a string o' glass beads, an' when I ask him 'bout dem, he laugh an' say: 'My dear little miss, I forgot todder night when I was at Mars Gus' store.

Jes you wait till I cut de ole rooster's spurs!
Den I'll sell him an' buy you de bes' string deir
is ; will you have yaller or blue ? '"

"Just like all men, Juno, they always forget.
Don't depend on them."

"If Dick tells me he's goin' ter giv' me any-
t'in', certain sure he'll buy it de fu's time massa
drives ter de store."

"Perhaps he is also buying for the other girls
in the same way. White and black, they will
all flirt !"

"Dick say he wouldn't buy a brass pin fer any
odder gal. Daniel promise Judy an' Peggy a
bundle o' candy, an' Judy is braggin' now 'bout
a real gol' pin he's goin' ter give her."

"Juno, tell me, do you know what people call
love? Does your heart ever thump or go pit-a
pat ? "

"Missy, you's makin' game o' me ! Eb'ry time
Dick drives de carriage ter de front dooe my
heart trembles like."

"I see only one way that I can help you. Go
and get a pencil and a sheet of paper. I'll write
Dick and Daniel; then you may draw names, as
you did when you became my maid. After so
much trouble in deciding, remember, you must be
content with the one you get.

No time was to be lost ; the excited girl real-

ised that her destiny was now about to be irrevo-
cably decided.   So casting aside her timidity, she
pleaded as if for her very life !

"Oh, my dear missy, don't make me draw
papers, caise I likes Dick lots better dan Daniel."

"Foolish girl ! Why then all this useless talk.
Couldn't you have told me at first that you loved
the coachman. Of course he is more suited to
you than a corn-field hand. In a day or two I
suppose you'll be asking for wedding clothes and
a feast.

"I's so happy, ma'am. Won't Dick be glad when
I tell him ter-night dat we is goin' ter git married.
Do buy me a w'ite wedden dress, a w'ite veil an'
w'ite flowers an' w'ite gloves ; you know Miss
Julia King is done buy lots of putty t'ings fer her
Sara what's goin' ter marry Uncle Jack's son,
Sam ; won't you give Dick dat coat an' pants
massa say he don't want ? an' in de bureau drawer
is a w'ite vest tear down de back an' a pair of old
w'ite gloves." She did not make one pause in
her long request.

Our coachman's beaming face, the next morning, clearly indicated that the engagement was
agreed on. And not waiting for orders, he asked,
as I entered the carriage, " Shall I drive to Mars
Gus' store, ma'am ? "

I looked at him, and suspecting what he was

thinking of, replied, "You may stop there after my call at Mrs. Rowland's."

On our homeward way Dick urged his horses more than was his wont. In his heart there was a longing to let it be known over the place that Juno's wedding clothes were bought. Daniel, of course, would hear the news, and would realize that this prize was lost to him.

As the carriage stopped at the gate, a smiling ginger-coloured face, from an upstairs window, looked out; Juno's heart was thumping wildly.

When her trousseau was finished, Saturday night was decided upon for the marriage. Early in the week preparations began.

"Both is of de household fam'ly," said Uncle Toby; "de big pot must be put in de leetle pot."

He spoke with authority, as he had been asked by Lydia to overlook the preliminary arrangements.

Accordingly, selecting twelve marriageable girls, he gave to each an egg, instructing them that at a given signal they must break them. "Min' you," said he, "the first wench what puts down her two half shells, keeping de yelk without marrin' it, by de law of fate must be de next one ter have a wedden feast."

About this circle of joyous egg-breakers a number of sturdy black fellows stood, wondering if they would stand as groom when the next cake was made.

At the end of the table Daniel, short of stature, peeped between Judy and Peggy, hoping one or the other would win.

In slavery days, Southern masters supplied all wedding feasts on their plantations with meat, flour, sugar, butter, and coffee; while friends of the couple deemed it their pleasure to give chickens and eggs.

Toby tried to see that supper was sufficient for everybody to have "a right smart bite," otherwise, he declared, "dar would neber be any chilluns."

Swansea, having no chapel, the wash-house was cleared of tubs, its walls decked with cedar boughs sprinkled with white-wash, and tufted with cotton fleece. Two men and two girls stood as waiters. It was so, in fact, that the expression, "When you get married, I'll wait on you," originated.

By eight o'clock the open fire-place was ablaze with resinous pine-knots. The room soon filled with guests, each bringing his or her own bench. In one corner was a soap-box covered with carpet. This was for the watchman, Frank, who had come from Green Forest to perform the ceremony.

"Dey is missy comin' now fer de w'ite veil," many whispered.

To ensure happiness at a negro wedding, the tarlatan veil must be arranged by white fingers.

Like all brides and grooms, both Juno and Dick tried to look their best. And any owner would have been proud of them. As Frank mounted the soap-box, a breathless silence reigned.

"Bro' Toby," said he, "will you see dat de man an' 'oman is jestly placed, deir right han's tightly clasped."

"Now, bredderen an' sisteren, let us pray fer de good estate of Israel. Blessed Lord, here is a'sembly congregate in dis house made wid hands ter witness de j'inin' of two of Israel chilluns. We t'ank de, O Fadder, dat dey both on dem is baptise chilluns of de chu'ch, sprinkled wid water blessed in de riber Jordan dat day when a dove come down.

"Send, O Lord, dis night, a blessin' ter rest on de head of dis pair. Wid one mouth we is prayin' dat so long as dey lives dey will neber forgit what dey is 'bout ter promise. Earthly love is teched deir heart. Lord, in dis solumn hour, burn deir understandin' wid a coal of fire, so dey kin neber 'bliterate from deir mind what dey's goin' ter say."

"Amen! amen!" passed from one to another.

Looking intently at the groom, he continued:

" Dick, my brudder, is you fully 'cided ter take dis lovely lady you's holdin' by de hand ter be your lawful weddin' wife ? "

" I is, sah ! "

" Is you sure you'll love her forever an' ever, better dan yourself ? "

" Yes, sah."

" Is you willin' ter cut wood, bring water, an' wait on um, not 'lone when she's sick, but when she's well ? "

" I is, sah."

With a touch of tenderness in his voice, Frank continued : " Juno, my sister, you hears dese good promises. Is you certain sure you loves dis man, squeezin' your han', better dan all de fellows galavantin' up an' down dis plantation ? " —he waved his hand over the crowd—" Is you made up your mind ter cook, patch, an' wash ? Is you willin' ter git up early o' cold mornin's, when de stars is yit a-twinklin', so he breakfast will be cooked t'rough an' t'rough ; not scorched on top ? Is you solumnly made up your mind ter obey dis man ter de best of your knowledge ? "

Toby caught a faint response, and exclaimed, " De lady say 'Yes'!"

" You both on you is now promised ; den in de name of de Lord an' de chu'ch I sarves, wid de consent of your massa an' missy, an' afore all dese people, I proclaims you both man an' wife. Hunno people, hear what de good book says "— he lifted Lydia's English Bible to his lips and kissed it—" What is j'ined by de Gods let not man or 'oman interfere wid ! "

Down from the soap-box he then stepped, laying his black hand upon the couple's white cotton gloves, that were in close touch.

" My brudder, take a bit of advice : When dis lady gits fractious, as all does sometimes, neglectin' your work, don't hit um like a no-count fellow, but jes you walk her straight ter your massa.   He's a good man, he'll set it right."

With still a ring of pathos in his tone, he turned to the bride : " Sister, some day you'll feel like grumbling ;—all does. Jes you shet your mouth tight, an' call to min' dis hour, when, like a necklace of roses, de yoke was put ober your head.   Roses has prickies, but dey is sweet an' purty.   Amen ! "

He remounted his box, and, lifting both hands, he enjoined: "Bredderen, wid one min' j'in me in supplication : ' Dear Lord Jesus, dis man an' he wife is 'clared in dis public 'sembly dat dey loves one anodder an' 'tends ter be faithful an' true ter todder.   We is now come ter de t'rone of Grace ter beg dat a blessed benediction will fall down an' settle on deir head like early dew, what keep corn fresh an' green. When de sun gits hot an' trouble comes, Lord, do hold dem like de apple of dy eye, in de hollow of dy hand. Amen!"

Bowing to the couple, he then said: "Will de gent'man salute he bride wid a holy kiss square in de mouth?"

The smack resounded from the four corners of the low ceiling.

"Amen! amen!" burst from the crowd.

Frank then spoke again: "Hunno people, by de gen'rosity of we good w'ite folks, outside is a table groanin' wid good eaten; after you has saluted de bride, you is 'vited ter de feast.

In imitation of her mistress, Juno had placed two five-cent pieces in her bride's cake. Her attendants, or waiters, cut for them. If a man should get it, he would hang it on his watchless chain. If a girl, she would hang in the centre of her string of bright glass beads.

The supper eaten, music and dancing followed.

Negro marriages were always on Saturday, friends on an adjoining plantation usually giving a dinner in their honor on Sunday. This, then, was their bridal tour.

XIII.

How Can We Let Missy Die?

"And statesmen at her council met
  Who knew the seasons when to take
  Occasion by the hand and make
The bounds of freedom wider yet."
                    —TENNYSON.

IN time, another cradle needed to be rocked. And who could sway it more gently than Lydia?

"Mommer's got 'nother heir," she said, clasping the tiny stranger to her bosom. "'Nother new-born child; 'nother master ter love an' ter take care of her when she's old. My sweet baby boy! I prays de Lord you'll be spared ter your mommer."

Southern plantation-life was not a Utopia, with days gliding by upon wings of ease. Sweet dreams of young married life were, on the contrary, often hampered by vexing cares. To keep order required a steady head. To produce a profitable crop, unremitting care. Men, women, and children needed to be clothed and fed, and growing youths required constant change in the patterns of their clothes.

Complaints frequently came to me: " Missy, jes look at my breeches! Aunt Clarinda mak' dem fer high-water time; dey is so tight I can't set down. My jacket won't button, an' I couldn't hug a gal wid it on."

Other boys had, then, to be put into these ill-fitting garments. Slaves, or negroes, too, not having the elastic constitution of factory work-ers, died suddenly from cold or exposure.

Doctors turn out of bed cheerfully, or at least promptly, for gold, but for a child-wife to do so because some old woman declared, "If missy didn't come she would die," seemed hard; yet their illness represented uninvested capital from which no interest accrued, with added expense of doctor and nurse. Therefore, self-interest prompted a care of the sick.

It mattered not what ailed a negro—pain in the head, body, or chest—the forehead invariably had to be bound with a band of white cloth; picturesque, it is true, but to them always sugges-tive of pain. They cured sore throat by tightly strapping a tuft of hair on the top of the head; lift-ing, thus, an obtrusive palate. Sighs and groans greeted us every morning: "I's so sick I kin hardly hold up my haid!"

Cæsar's delight was to empty the contents of a castor-oil bottle down his capacious throat. My husband and I have spent hours and hours at night beside ill men or women, not daring to leave the giving of medicine to a nodding granny.

As may be expected, shamming was not unusual. Lydia, in fact, often spoke of two instances. Jed, a negro seamstress of an old lady living near Green Forest, hearing of a basket of pinafores to be finished, came one morning with her right hand encased in a meal-poultice. She said she had been roused from sleep by a sudden pain.

Home-remedies failing, a physician was summoned. He found neither splinter, rising, nor any symptom of erysipelas; but her will closed her fingers, and nothing could relax the muscles. Thereafter, her life was a state of supreme leisure, her arm slung to her shoulder. Lydia and her children often caught sight of her open fingers; but she carried a cake-canister key, and so their lips were sealed. Her hand remained closed until the shackles of slavery were snapped.

Lydia, with her "w'ite chilluns," sometimes visited old Silvia, bedridden for twenty years.

Her master, a physician, tried exercise in a hoop suspended from the ceiling, but, left alone, Silvia tumbled to the floor in a lump, her spine seeming not strong enough to keep her erect. But, for that matter, with her desire to collapse, no power on earth could have prevented it.

Her master finally left off all experiments, making her surroundings as comfortable as possible. During the war he died, but old Silvia was cared for still, and seemed quite reconciled to her long confinement.

When the news of freedom reached her, she arose with full power over her legs and spine ; for she had kept them supple by walking at night, while her owners slept. Many negroes knew of her deception, but they feared to inform on her, lest they be treated to a cup of cold poison that she kept concealed.

Both pleasures and trials surrounded us, and so months doubled into years. In Lydia's cabin there was peace, if not happiness; and Robin drifted into "a husband of no importance."

Every one living north of Mason and Dixon's line, without regard to colour, gloried in their freedom.

South of that latitude thousands wore the yoke of slavery.

Stephen A. Douglas and other agitators, wishing to extend the boundary of slave-owning states, waxed hot in discussion. Men delegated to make and amend laws in the Capitol at Wash-

ington, now set their constituency a bad example;
reason lost sway; for members on the same sena-
torial benches flew at each other with fiery, hasty
words. Sermons and political speeches resounded
with the keynote, " Set the negro free! Colonise
them in Liberia!" Abolition zeal waxed hot,
and many negroes were shipped to their native
country. Sambo and Cudgo, however, worked
their way home, preferring, they said, bondage
with clothing and civilisation, to freedom in
Liberia.

Since Captain Hawkins venturesome purchase
in 1620, years had passed. Smouldering fires
now began to break forth. Under the Stars and
Stripes, a glorious union was in danger of being
rent asunder. Eventually, our lovely southern
homes were engulfed and destroyed, like Pom-
peii of old, with crumbling walls and heaps of
ashes to mark the spots.

Of the civil war the merest thread will be given,
and only as it affected the life of both Lydia and
Marlborough.

South Carolina seceded December 2d, 1860,
declaring herself capable of governing her own
State affairs. Others followed. Jefferson Davis,
of Mississippi, was subsequently elected President
of the Confederacy, and Richmond, Virginia,
named as its Capital.

A standing army and navy, commanded by officers from West Point and Annapolis, supported by a powerful government at Washington, able instantly to mass and reinforce her troops, should have intimidated a young Confederacy, restricted in materials of warfare and with a wide area over which to disperse her men.   But with the words, "Andaces fortuna Juvat," a cry rang wildly over the south, "To arms! to arms!"   Men and boys buckled on their accoutrements, and, with kisses and words of encouragement from wives, mothers, sisters and sweethearts still warm on their lips, banded into companies and regiments, rushing to the front, hoping to return wearing the victor's crown.

Southern gentlemen stuck their heels higher than their heads, smoke curling from the finest of Havana cigars, and laughed at the impudence of northern statesmen : " Let the —— Yankees come, we can whip them; batter down any barrier ; blow up any gunboat daring to interfere on our seacoast."

The first cannon was fired from Fort Sumter in this spirit.

Letha and I had spent many a Saturday holiday there, with General Edward C. Anderson.

Our country " flowed with milk and honey," and money was plentiful.   The soil was red with iron ore. But no one ventured to dig for richer gains, content with its surface-yield of cotton.

Living in sunny rooms adjoining "Uncle Tom's Cabin," few negroes surmised why white people fought. Lydia listened with interest to details in newspapers, never dreaming, however, that her master would leave his family for the battle-field.

In the south, as well as in the north, breakfast on Sunday is alway late; and in ante-bellum days it was luxuriously so. The presence too of war in nowise caused any well-to-do southerner to modify this custom. One Sunday Revilo and I were standing on the front piazza, in the spring sunshine, listening to a pet canary, that vied with wild birds in their morning song; the air was perfumed with roses, and on every side ducks and chickens quacked, clucked, and scratched, regard-less of this day of rest.

Edward appeared at the front door. In his hand he held a long peacock brush. He then scraped first one, then the other, bare foot, touched his forelock, and said, "Missy, massa, ma say de vittals is on de table pipin' hot."

Hardly was the blessing said, when the boy bounded to the front window, exclaiming "Law! yonders Mars Charley wid all he regiments on; an' it's Sunday too!"

11

Every one rushed to the garden gate,—fly-brush as well.

Reining in his horse the young officer shouted: "Meet us at Barnard's landing,—Yankee gunboats are steaming up the Riseburg!"

Having discharged his first active duty, he wheeled his horse, and disappeared.

"My husband uttered a shrill whistle, which was answered promptly by Dick. "Saddle Romeo at once, with my cavalry saddle; be ready in your uniform to mount Juliet and go with me."

He ran up the garden-walk and up the stairs, two steps at a bound, and quickly donned a gray fatigue uniform. With a word of cheer to me, he leaped into his saddle, waved an adieu at the avenue gate, and was gone.

Joy and happiness had dwelt in our home; now it appeared shrouded with approaching death and separation. Quick firing guns and cannon drowned the song of birds and the cackle of poultry. Edward resumed his post, manfully fighting greedy and pestiferous flies; Lydia stood at the steps holding in her arms our crowing baby; Juno, with a plate of hot waffles, found the table deserted; so she looked about and joined those at the front gate; Maria, the cook, hearing confusion, rushed through the house with hot fluffy biscuits for her master.

He was gone,—his pockets bulging with carbine ammunition. Mute with amazement, no one spoke until Juno screamed, " Missy's w'ite as a ghos'." Kind insensibility released the tension, and I fell to the ground.

Runners rushed to the village for doctor or friends. Not a white man was to be found. The clergyman even was absent ; for with sermon in hand, he was on his way to Barnard's landing.

" What is we to do ? We can't let missy die, an' massa's away," the negroes cried.

Lydia stroked my brow, and did her best to console. " Don't min' dat rumblin' ; in spring dere is always t'under in de air,"—yet not a cloud obscured the sky,—" you couldn't hear shootin' at Barnard's landin' ; dat's way down by Pleasant Grove chu'ch."

Bowl after bowl of gruel, during the day, was sent to my bedside : " Beg missy to take one spoonful fer Chloe, Clarinder, or Peggy," each said, respectively.

In its circuit the sun traveled down, down below the horizon. No word of the exaggerated accounts of the killed and wounded were repeated upstairs. At nightfall the firing ceased. After tucking " her baby boy " in bed, Lydia snored in a rocking-chair. Juno nodded beside my bed, intermittently brushing away mosquitoes.

A sound of horses' hoofs came. "Massa's safe," a chorus of voices shouted. "Massa's safe, t'ank de Lord!"

"Massa's safe ag'in," cried Dick; "but Mars Charley's stiff daid, dem Yankees shot him t'rough an' t'rough de heart. We is licked de Yankees, Massa's comin' home in de mornin'. We is whipped de Yankees? Hurrah! hurrah!"

Excited voices of the negroes took up the refrain.

Lydia spread for herself a pallet beside the crib, bidding Juno do the same in the hall.

I slept, and dreamed that Revilo had returned untouched by a bullet. In my joy I extended my arms and clasped my husband round his neck. I awoke! He had returned; and, without rousing maid or nurse, was actually leaning over me, listening to my murmur of joy.

I am sure that similar scenes took place all over Siberty County that fair Sunday, when, for the first time, many men and boys faced belching cannon.

In feverish expectancy we awaited our newspaper. The columns were full of accounts of the bombarding of Fort Sumter. Later news came of bloodshed elsewhere. The paper reported, also, "Yankees and Rebels are at it like cats and dogs."

Southerners firmly believed that England, our "mother country," would interfere. To prevent a cotton famine in her land she must interpose. And though many wails of distress arose in Lancashire, and other English factory-districts, not a finger did Great Britain lift. We soon realised that we had to rely solely upon ourselves and our own meagre resources.

Battle succeeded battle. The Monitor and Merrimac had their say;—defeat, victory, cannon, and soldiers changed positions.

History has shown that the most bitter and also the most hopeful in this unnatural strife were women. Lydia could not be reconciled to her master going to the front. And when, owing to failing sight, he was ordered home, no one rejoiced more than she at his return to Swansea.

It is a well-known fact that southern officers and men went to camp attended by one or more of their slaves. Chim sent Marlborough with her brother Fleming, a captain of cavalry; she hoped that the change of scene and excitement of army life would rouse him from the lethargy into which he had lapsed after Lydia's marriage in the nursery. His assistant, Amos, Lily's eldest son, enjoyed the tramp, tramp of soldiers and the beating of drums, and his merry whistle sounded in the woods where his master's horses were tethered.   Flourishing an old cavalry pistol, minus a lock, he was more self-important than the general in command.   Many messages reached his girl at home : " Don't be dancin' wid no 'count fellows, 'fore long we is goin' ter lick de Yankees, den I'll come wid a cockade in my hat.   You'll be proud ter hang on ter de arm of a real live soldier."

XIV.

An Indian War Dance.

"Wherefore I hold him best at ease
That lives content with his estate."
RICHARD CARLETON.

SHERMAN'S onward march to the sea made it necessary for us to quit Swansea: partial blindness would not protect Revilo from capture. We, therefore, left Maria and her husband Will in charge of our house and its effects.

Lydia hurriedly packed two trunks, and we left for Mason, where my sisters had gone for safety. Then the plantation negroes, with their master (he the only white person) started through the country for western Georgia.

In Revilo's heart there was no thought of fear to intensify the hardships of camping at night. His so-called "driven slaves" guarded and cared for him with tenderness.

In a wild and barren section they settled a home. Cutting down young pines, they peeled off the outer bark, under which were often found the deadly chaintail scorpion.

To shelter a large force was no easy matter, and building cabins without even one nail made the labour more difficult. Merrily singing round a blazing log-heap, women and boys whittled wooden pins,—as substitutes for nails. Clapboards were then skilfully hung one over another on rough-hewn pine-rafters.

In that country a fire-brick had never been seen, yet each cabin needed to have a chimney. These were built of sticks and daubed with clay, in real pine-hut fashion. Snugly housed, our negroes joyfully undertook to build a larger cabin for me their absent mistress, their master encouraging them to use their best skill.

Alas! window glass was as scarce as nails. One small opening in the side had before it a wooden-pinned clapboard shutter. A door similarly constructed hung on wooden hinges, its only inside fastening, an oaken latch, controlled by a swaying cotton cord from the outside.

Revilo now wrote, asking us to leave Mason for our future home.

To me it had been a joy to see my sisters safe, and Lydia was jubilant at meeting Old Soul and many of the children of her former fellow-labourers, who were removed to Mason for safety.

Chim, with her little son, was there, and Letha, too, with her fatherless infant.

On Saturday night before we left, a sad occurrence spread a gloom over every one. A negro lad with a blind eye and partly deaf, was shot while stealing potatoes from a one-legged soldier; these yams were all the soldier had to keep wife and children from starving.

Israel the lad told, on his deathbed, how a black man gave him a Confederate bill to help him fill a bag at the potato bank. "Beg de Lord ter pardon you, Israel," Lydia pleaded. "Mars C. C. say when we is in earnest de God in heaven hears we cry."

The wounded boy replied: "I is, aunt Lyddy. I is so sorry. Don't you 'member how Sam'l call de Lord, an' he answer, 'Here is me, Sam'l?'"

The spark of divine truth, grasped by him in the wash-house Sunday-school, led him to the foot of the cross. Tuesday, in a drizzling rain that froze into sparkling crystals on the trees, his body was borne to the graveyard in a rude pine coffin, blackened with diluted soot. Frank, the watchman, was not there, but a coloured Baptist preacher offered a prayer, with words of warning to his young companions who peered into the yawning grave.

The next day we started for the pineland home, where the season of planting corn was at its height. The negroes often asked, " How will missy live in de log-pen, not so good as de poorest cabin at Green Forest or Swansea ? "

On Thursday, after a wearisome drive of fourteen miles over a sandy road, we neared our destination. Shadows dim and dimmer outlined themselves as the wind lazily sighed in pine needles overhead.

In a tumble-down vehicle, the jogging trot of two mules lulled our party into sleepy unconsciousness. Dick roused himself occasionally, to cluck to his stubborn team. Lydia nodded, with " her baby boy " in her arms, forgetting that she would soon see her husband. Turning a sharp curve in the country road, a dazzling glare suddenly roused us from dreams and reveries.

" Indians ! " I cried, muffling my voice ; " there are a tribe of Indians dancing their war dance. See ! their feathers are waving above the flaming torches ! Turn quickly, Dick, and drive for your life. If they see us, we will all be scalped. Oh ! why did we leave Swansea ? We would have been better treated by the Yankees than by these wild devils."

Lydia leaned out of one window ; her master out the other ; while our tired mules stood stock-

still, backing their long ears, their tails upright in
fright over such an unusual sight.   A shout rent
the air as the smoke lifted ; and as the fantastic
dancers caught a glimpse of our carriage, they
shot forward.

Lydia screamed, " Ain't no Injins ; it's we
people.   Dey is Uncle Sawney wid a burnin'
light'ood knot.   Wake up, my 'baby-boy,' we
niggars is come ter welcome deir little massa."
Joyous as a school-girl, she greeted one after the
other.

In concert, the negroes then joined in a favourite
plantation-song :

> "Come love, come,
> De boat lies low,
> She lies high an' dry
> On de Ohio."

At the new cabin, women lifted me through its
door.   No room ever looked more attractive.
Upon its rough-hewn log floor, covered with dry
wire grass, was stretched a carpet, the pattern
identical with one at Swansea.   On the clay-
daubed wall hung two familiar pictures.   Pine
logs blazed and snapped, and on each side of the
large fire-place stood two empty rocking-chairs
and a child's arm-chair.

Ephraim never could be likened to an unturned cake before that blaze; for, in self-defense, he would shift his position.

The sweet perfume of roses makes one confident that roses are near; so, at this unexpected sight of rocking-chairs, carpet and pictures, I knew love and devotion surrounded us. Our negroes left Swansea in a desperate hurry, expecting daily the arrival of the enemy. Revilo afterward told me that it was with difficulty he could make them put essential food and clothing into the wagons, so determined they were that their absent mistress should have a few of her former comforts. Under these trying and unusual circumstances their actions left no doubt of their true devotion.

Lydia named this home Pine Knot, because the clapboard door was covered with rough knots. One room was furnished as parlour and dining-room, with a rude pine table, pinned together with wooden pins; placed around it were benches similar to aunt Sallie's Sunday-school seat; not, indeed, ever likely to make one loiter in the hope of courses,—not to be served. A frisky young mule's heels had shattered a barrel of china, packed at Swansea; we, therefore, now used blue plates, brown cups, and white saucers: each, too, of different shape, and belonging mostly to Lydia and Juno.

Outward appearances mattered little to us, so
long as our appetites were appeased. Of water
and wood there was no lack. Dried blackberry
and strawberry leaves, steeped, supplied us with
tea. Juno brewed coffee from parched rye and
acorn kernels. Lydia made "her boy's" tea of
milk and water, without sugar.

This, in truth, embittered her against the Yankees more than ever.

With Confederate money, bank-notes, and even
gold we could not procure necessary food; nor
yet raiment. We did grow sufficient corn, or
maize, to ward the wolf from our door; yet with
neither salt nor soda, and very little butter, food
was tasteless. Sawney churned what butter we
did have, by shaking a black bottle up and down,
till the thin milk from our wire-grass-fed cow con-
gealed or thickened into a white, frothy substance.
Even the keenest appetite found dry cornbread
tasteless, served as it was three times daily, accompanied but seldom with a rasher of poor,
smelly bacon. Without salt in a hot climate,
beef would not keep. Like the Indians, we
"jerked it."

Juno did her best in the kitchen, grumbling
meanwhile because the Yankees did not let her
have soda; her master, she said, always paid cash
for what he bought. Simple-hearted Juno! The

restrictions of a blockade were too profound for
her untutored mind.   My limited knowledge of
chemistry, however, added greatly to Juno's happiness, when I showed her how to lighten corn-
bread with corn-cob ashes.   The thought is suggestive of grit, I admit, yet the alkaline liquid,
mixed with a watery butter-milk, greatly improved
the corn-bread.

At the first experiment Juno screamed with delight, calling, " Ma, you an' aunt Clarinda jes
come an' peep in de oven ; de corn bread is a
spillin' over de pan."

She could scarcely wait till the browning, so
great was her desire to sample the loaf.   Poultry
required time to multiply, of course, and ours,
also, were too well bred to sleep in log coops,
preferring tree-limbs instead.   The pine forest
was alive with hawks and owls, and so, while they
feasted on poultry, we ate dry bread.   " Frizzle-
top," one of our finest hens, made for herself a
nest on the earthen floor of our dairy.   I kept a
strict account of her eggs, but day after day one
disappeared.

Lydia then took the matter in hand.   She was
determined to find out who was stealing these
eggs, suspecting her son Edward.

Howls from behind her cabin, and a broken
birch flourishing in her hand, later told the story.

"I sees yaller marks 'bout your mouth! Is you forgot how Israel is all turned ter decompose, all caise he took potatoes what wa'n't his. I means ter t'rash you eb'ry time you eats an aigg."

"Ma, I's innocent," protested the boy, "you ask missy if I eat dem aiggs. She has eyes all round her head, an' sees eb'ry blessed t'ing I does."

But Lydia was unconvinced.

The mystery was solved, however, when Dick killed, near the dairy, a house-snake, and, severing it, in the centre, out burst an egg in perfect shell, with another partly digested.

Edward clapped his hands with delight, saying : "It's always so. I gits all de lickin'; de snake de good eatin'."

Food was not our only want; for scarcely a day passed but some one asked, "When is we ter git new clothes?"

"Missy," Cæsar said, "my old 'oman Chloe is patch an' patch; now she's cut off my coat-tail fer seat my breeches. All my life I's been a ladies' man; de best beau on de place; but now I's shame fer go 'mongst de gals; dey laughs at my coat widout any tail, an' my cowhides wid cypress soles makes such a racket, folks is got no chance ter steal a kiss."

Not a negro woman at Pine Knot understood

the art of carding and spinning, nor yet of weaving. We therefore engaged Mrs. Johns, "a cracker" living near by, to come and teach Juno and others.

The term "cracker"—applied to poor whites—comes from their habit of walking beside small carts cracking a long whip. And no greater insult could be offered to a negro than to compare him to a "poor cracker." "Buckra," meaning rich white folks, originated in Africa, where Mungo Park was called by the natives the "good buckra man."

We were fortunate in being able to get two pairs of cards and a spinning wheel. But money could not obtain a loom; no one would part with theirs. Pine-land crackers suddenly found a market for home-woven cloth.

Unable to buy a loom, then, our only recourse seemed to be that of making one. This we did; first, by constructing a miniature model in cornstalks, pinned together with lightwood splinters, instead of nails or tacks. Our carpenter was not skilled in work outside the usual line of plantation cabin-building, but, with failures and trials, we did, eventually, get a loom, with all its intricate trappings. Possessed of a loom, with hanks upon hanks of homespun cotton-thread, we were yet as far from the art of weaving cloth as ever.

Mrs. Johns, in consideration of a roll of paper money, came to give Juno her first lesson,—sizing the thread.

Having dismounted and tethered her " critter," she left it to graze on wire-grass ; she then threw back over her shoulders the front ends of a three-cornered shawl, worn persistently on the hottest day in summer or on the coldest in winter. Her split-board bonnet, tied under her chin, went, with one shove, to the "waterfall" of her hair, disclosing a leathery thick skin. It was of the same dirty sallow colour of all "cracker" women throughout the country, although these sun-protectors should have ensured a fair complexion ; for they are never removed except to be supplanted by a nightcap.

Juno was on a broad grin during the entire lesson ; for "crackers" were unaccustomed to servants.

"Gin I come ag'in be you sure ter have these cob-spools well covered!" said Mrs. Johns.

Alas, when she came the second time no reel had been burned through the center.

" You stupid, dingy, black, ginger-coloured niggars," she said, with a scowl, " didn't you know dose cobs had ter go on ter de warpin' bars? "

We did not.

The cabin that was built for the loom was now

12

a place of great interest. Day after day we
watched the cloth increase, the click, click, of a
hand-swung shuttle making novel and unusual
music. Juno, happily, manifested such excellence
in weaving that she left the kitchen to reign
supreme at the loom.

Our negroes were not alone in their needs; for
our own garments showed the wear and tear of
time. Ten, twenty, fifty-dollar Confederate bills
were plentiful; but no paper signed by Jefferson
Davis, and guaranteed by his government, could,
alas, cover protruding elbows and knees.

Our slaves fared better than we; they still had
frocks of Green Forest's dead mistress for Sunday
clothes. And how they delighted to flaunt their
flounces on festive occasions! This habit, too, of
giving to them half-worn gowns enhanced, doubtless, their love for furbelows and gewgaws. Mid-
dle-aged negro women always laid aside one gown
to be used as a burial robe. Nothing could re-
voke the doom when once a dress was dedicated
to the tomb.

Chloe's thrift in patching her husband's garments suggested to me the idea of renovating my
worn sleeves and bodices. Like the last rose of
summer, one Sunday frock now hung alone on a
wooden peg of our clay-daubed wall. The attic
at Swansea could have supplied me with many

beautiful bits, had the house and all it contained been other than a heap of ashes.

On Lydia's cabin-cleaning day, she spread all her belongings upon the grass to sun.

Surprised, I asked, " Have you that byadier silk dress yet?" " I have never seen you wear it."

" No ma'am ; I's never put it on ; it's my bu'ial robe."

" Lydia, it's just the thing to make my old gray silk perfect. I'll give you a new one-hundred dollar Confederate bill for it."

" Uncle Toby, what knows, says ef you changes your mind 'bout coffin-clothes you'll sure ter die. Please, missy, don't ask me fer it ; I ain't ready ter leave 'my baby boy ;' he couldn't get along widout his mommer."

Neatly folded, the byadier dress was put into her chest, with an old English inlaid snuff-box her mother had left her, an heirloom of her master, Squire Jameston.

Orchards blossomed into full leaf again ; winter birds cast their sombre hues ; and their brilliant plumage flashed in the sun. Thus, nature seemed making ready to join in a glad Easter morning.

More than one southern woman that Eastertide sighed over her inability to wear a new gown on Easter Sunday. In the first part of Holy week Dick and his master drove to Halby. On their return, forgetting his tired mules, stamping at the gate, Dick awaited the opening of a store-bundle he had deposited upon the dining-room table : " It's fer you, missy," he said, and his wide-spread mouth showed his delight.

"Ten yards of heavy Osnaburg for me!" I exclaimed, showing as great joy as a child over its first wax doll. "You paid sixty dollars a yard ! What a lovely gift !" That Easter Sunday birds and flowers had a rival in our log church.

Lydia never gave her daughter any peace until there was cloth woven for a new suit for her master. It was made of wool drawn from the edge of our mattress—cotton put in its place. A concoction, made of herbs, dyed the warp and woof a brown tint. Five women *kept* this secret.

One Saturday night new trousers, waistcoat, and coat hung on a wooden pin, in place of thread-bare garments.

A spirit of friendly jealousy arose the next day at church, when the home-made garments were examined, much to the annoyance of the wearer, who vowed never to don another home-made suit. Paying, as we did, six hundred dollars for one dress, is it surprising that pockets were empty of both handkerchiefs and gloves? It seemed fashionable to be without them.

Hair-pins were as few as hairs upon " Uncle Ned's head."

Finding a bit of wire, our negro men bent and ground it into shape, giving Lydia the pleasure of presenting me with a dozen hair pins; hand-made and most valuable, it is true, but pulling uncomfortably my hair. Needles and pins were scarce, and a diamond brooch seemed not more valuable than a steel needle, capable of dragging after it, through hand-loom cloth, a length of home-spun thread.

Lydia's next ambition was to have fine material woven for " her boy's " first knee-pants.

With a goose-quill dipped into soot, previously mixed with molasses, we wrote letters on scraps of wall paper, thus keeping in touch with sorrow-ing friends. At that date nearly every one was weeping for some kinsman. Envelopes we cut from the same figured paper, and sealed them with gum that had exuded from peach or plum-trees. There was not a spoonful of flour in our larder for paste, nor for food.

Newspapers reached us occasionally, printed on the reverse side of the same nondescript flow-ered wall-paper.

Housewives of the south daily taxed their ingenuity to supply immediate wants. They were allied to their sisters, the five foolish virgins, having no oil for lamps.

A burning resinous pine-knot seemed our only way of dispelling the darkness of night. In August, too! Sawney gained permission to go to the sea-coast, where he boiled hard berries of the sea-myrtle, and, to our delight, returned with a fine cake of sea-green wax. Not a neighbour possessed a candle-mould ; and, of course, workers in tin were at the front, baring their breasts to cannon balls.

We dipped yard-lengths of twisted cotton-thread into this melted wax, and, when ready to light it, wound it round the neck of a black bottle, one end erect. This served for candle and candle-stick.

The friction of flint and steel took the place of matches.

Peruvian bark from swamps gave us needed quinine.

Every one planted poppies, the creamy juice exuding from green seed-pods when pierced, being really opium in its crude state. The perfumed leaves of the Queen of flowers we gathered for druggists' compounds.

The Government allowed but one physician to every twenty square miles, and, as may be supposed, he was in great demand. Indeed, a messenger for one often travelled in vain from house to house.

There was little medicine save concoctions made from herbs, the component parts of which southern women soon learned to know.

Nothing was wasted; salt brine even, from fish or meat, was boiled and clarified with egg-shells. This process precipitated a fine salt, much prized for table use.

Our teeth decayed indiscriminately. Dentists were in the army. Sufferers endured hours of anguish, their faces muffled in scorched cotton.

Negroes will not bear toothache. A tooth that ached had to be extracted.

And so Sawney, when hurriedly leaving Swansea, put into the wagon a massive pair of forceps.

When Lydia heard that Sawney was about to extract a great molar, she was always present with her little master, to see the fun and give advice:

"Be sure you stick dat tooth in de chimney-jam, else your truck patch ain't no 'count fer peas or beans, caise Bro' Toby say it's de Gospel truth dat Bro' Rabbit an' Bro' Wolf once on a time had a big quarrel 'bout teeth. Bro' Wolf, grinnin', laughed at Bro' Rabbit's little teeth."

"Den Bro' Rabbit he squat on he hind legs an' answer: 'You needn't be a-braggin'. If I's a min' ter, I kin show teeth bigger dan you has. ' "

" ' You stuck-up w'ite-tail varmin,' said Bro' Wolf, ' fer eb'ry tooth bigger dan mine you bring me'—an' he open he jaw wide—' I'll pull out a palin' in a truck patch so you kin eat a good supper.'

" Bro' Rabbit found lots of nigger teeth in de trash heap 'long side de cabin ; so deir was many a truck patch eat up of nights."

The art of tanning leather was not understood in the south, but inasmuch as negroes could work well and comfortably without shoes, they felt no deprivation in having to go without foot-wear. But hats they must have, to protect them from a broiling summer sun. It was then by a happy chance that we discovered that wire-grass was suitable for this need.

Lydia, too, recalled having seen her old mother Nancy steep the ends of a gobbler's tail in hot water, after threading them in the order in which they grew. The softened quills were then easily compressed, and spread into fan-shape.

This luxury we greatly needed in our log church, where Sunday after Sunday we listened to two sermons, each an hour long. Many a day the thermometer would have registered ninety-nine and a half degrees in the shade, had we had such a thing.

Our one young gobbler at Pine Knot, who seemed as fond of a strut as a Hyde Park beau, now stalked or circled about his hens just as bravely without his appendage. His tail did sacrificial duty in church; getting me, too, into unmeasured trouble. For, thereafter, messenger after messenger came to Pine Knot with turkey feathers, saying, " Missy is pull out we gobbler tail; she say won't you make um into a fan gin next Sunday? "

At other times the quills were sent with a strip of wall paper attached. It read: "So sorry to trouble you. I have done my best and failed; please, will you finish this fan, for your loving friend? "

Love-work does not always pay. The more considerate, however, sent me either a brace of partridges,—caught in a trap,—a bit of home-tanned sheep-skin, or a comb of wild honey.

No one, it is true, at this period, was wearing silken gloves of ease.

How great a thing it is not to be miserable when skies grow black, and to be content with one's lot!

XV.

The Parson's Dagger.

"Grief and joy and hope and fear
Play their pageants everywhere."

LYDIA looked forward to the arrival of the post with breathless interest. The newspapers gave detailed lists of killed and wounded. "T'ank God Mars Flem's name is not deir," she exclaimed more than once, " but don't you t'ink it's strange dey neber says one word 'bout Bro' Molbro? I reckon he must be well, or dey would put his name down too."

Letters from our brother, the captain, in Virginia, often deplored the despondent moods that still oppressed Marlborough. He offered to let him return home, but his faithful servant refused, lest his master should be ill or wounded. No word or message came for Lydia; and this she could not understand. Handing me letters received months before, she would say, " Read dese ag'in, missy." " Read it careful, caise deir ought ter be one word fer me. Sure Bro' Molbro ain't forgot me when I prays fer him eb'ry night."

Owing to his solemn demeanor in camp Marlborough was known as the " Parson." No one had ever seen him spread his mouth save in a kind of half-smile. Two soldiers started a rumour that " the parson " carried in his waistcoat front a picture that he often kissed.

A picket squad, lazily joking around a camp fire, waiting for active duty, authorized themselves to ferret out this secret ; for, no trophy, no sentiment, was too sacred among such a set of men. The deputized band surrounded " the parson," and demanded the contents of his vest pockets.

Feeling sure that his refusal would be followed by force, Marlborough, like a Chesterfield, withdrew his military coat and his waistcoat, handing them to a sergeant. His look of pain half inclined the officer to return the garments unsearched. Curiosity, however, screwed to its highest pitch, must needs be satisfied ; nor could they forego the fun of examining his pockets. The sergeant, who had received the waistcoat, turned one pocket after another wrongside out.

From the first tumbled a jack-knife, with but a fragment of blade ; from the next, a roll of paper wrapped about a broken darning needle.

" You don't mend clothes with this," said one

man. "Why, it's rusty and broken; looks too as if it came out of the Ark. Is this the picture you've been kissing?" and he unfolded the paper,

"See here, boys, 'the parson' is partial to hoopskirts," laughed the sergeant.

"There's another pocket in the lining," and a soldier stepped forward, tapping the waistcoat. As he pulled the lining out, there sparkled in the sunlight a plain gold ring, held in place by strong stitches.

"L-y-d-i-a, Lydia! That's the lettering inside! Hurrah, hurrah, boys! Now we have the name of his gal! Lydia! Was it she who sold purple and fine linen, according to Bible accounts? Parson, is your Lydia young? Aren't you afraid she'll forget you while you're soldiering?"

"Stop, boys, don't tease him. I've a fellow-feeling for him, because it may be the ring of a dead wife. I'm a widower, too, parson; but don't you despair, when you get home there'll be lots of women glad to marry you with your plume of victory waving in your hat. Take my advice: it don't pay to grieve. Tell me, have you never laughed since your wife died?"

Marlborough, with genuine old-fashioned negro deference for white persons, stood in his shirt-sleeves awaiting the return of his waistcoat.

Touching his forelock, he replied: "T'ank you, gen'men fer your interest in me, but so far as I knows my wife Flora is still livin' at Mars Joe Lamont's plantation."

One by one the frolic-loving soldiers sneaked away, heartily ashamed of having demanded the contents of the "parson's" pockets.

General Grant was then marching onward to the sea, and Sherman's tents whitened our sun-kissed sea-shore. Many of our palatial homes were in ruins, and the great pulse-throb of the Confederacy was growing feeble—hope seemed gasping its last breath.

Revilo, requiring the skill of an oculist, left Pine Knot, to be gone a week. He called Belfast, the foreman, before starting, and said, "I leave my little family to your care."

Torrents of rain fell, overflowing the creeks that surrounded our place, isolating us; in truth, our nearest neighbour lived five miles away.

As may be supposed, my days were weary enough; but the nights, alas, were absolutely unbearable, with neither a lamp nor a book to shorten the tedium of oppressive darkness. Sewing was a task, rather than a pleasure; our half-worn garments had to be mended with home-spun thread; forced, too, into the eye of a needle three sizes too fine; and its point blunt. My gold thimble was worn into holes by heavy work, and my treasured needle sometimes left its eye in the tip of my finger, greatly exasperating me.

Lydia was within calling distance at night, yet she insisted that, during her master's absence, she should sleep beside "her boy's" couch.

" No one has ever molested us; why should they now; If anything happens, I will scream for you," said I.

Covering the chubby hands of her little master with kisses, she said good-night : "Sleep, baby, sleep sweet, till mommer comes in de mo'nin'. I 's a spoonful of 'lasses fer your tea."

About midnight Carlo's bark startled me from sleep; then I heard stealthy steps advance toward our shrunken wooden-pinned door : through the crevice the button within could easily be turned.

There are times in every one's life when seconds seem quadrupled. There was no bell-rope to pull; to scream would but increase anxiety by rousing a sleeping boy. Were we to be murdered in cold blood? The child, at least, would be spared consciousness. In the pines, hooting owls sounded their dismal notes of wailing, yet, strangely enough, sleep overcame me. At early morn Lydia's voice roused me : " Who's been in

dis cabin wid heavy shoes?" her screams for
her brother Belfast hurrying our negroes to the
cabin, eager to know if missy was safe.

On the piazza, by my door, were shoe-tracks
made by damp sand. The negroes declared,
"Dese is Yankee tracks; none of we folks has
such nails in deir shoes. Bro' Daniel was tellin'
last night 'bout two mens wid brass buttons in
de woods."

"I did see dem; dey call ter me; but I broke
an' run. Dey p'int deir guns at my head."

Sawney, Daniel's father, with a grave voice,
now spoke: "Hunno people, don't you bodder
wid blue-coats; dey tell too many lies. I hears
we is all ter git a mule an' forty acres o' land.
You know dat's a lie."

Belfast then snapped the trigger of an old gun
that stood in the dining-room: "If I had a load
of shot an' powder I'd show dose fellows what's
what; dey comin' here while massa's away!"

Lydia spread her pallet that evening beside the
bed of her white child; while I braced the benches
and rocking-chairs against the door.

"Go to sleep, missy," urged Lydia, "you'll
wake my boy; nobody kin put der finger on you
an' I here."

Her every word in childhood was implicitly
believed. But not now. What could she do in

the face of able-bodied men, as their shoe-tracks had shown them to be ?

Sleep for me seemed a lost factor. With un-defined apprehension, I waited. Suddenly I screamed, " Lydia wake up ! there's a step outside. Be quick ! call for Belfast. Oh, God ! to be murdered like this ! "

The nurse raised up on her elbow, saying, " Do, Miss Dodo, be quiet ! You know dey is no danger an' I is here."

I was beyond her control. Even ghostly visit-ors, summoned by her cabalistic words, could not keep me quiet now. I sprang to my feet; she too quickly rose and tried to soothe my fears, holding me fast in her arms. " It's we people," she whis-pered, " a keepin' guard ; dey 'greed ter take hour by hour till massa come home."

Imprisoned though we were by fordless creeks, we were still, as she declared, well guarded by slave-sentinels, doing voluntary night duty. Never king or queen could boast of more disin-terested love.

Some days thereafter each man received a gift.

" T'ank you, massa, but it's not fer money we kep' watch," they assured Revilo. " We promised ter take care of missy, an' we's done de best we knowed how."

The next day, at noon, the front gate opened

and two men in blue coats, with brass buttons, walked to the log steps. As if weary, they seated themselves. In a moment our house-servants surrounded me.

"What do you wish?" I asked; "are you ill?"

"Hungry, ma'am, hungry," said the younger, both looking pale and feeble. "Do give us a bit of bread; we haven't had a morsel since these nasty creeks overflowed. This is the most God-forsaken country I was ever in, and my friend here is dying, with not a drop of whisky or medicine to give him. Not even a pinch of salt to season what we can kill or steal. There's no use telling you a lie, we have stolen,"—he glanced up to where a string of red peppers hung against the logs. "Some nights ago we tried to reach those; we thought they were onions. There ain't one blamed mouthful in this place to seize," he continued. "I'm sure I can't see how you live. We took some corn, but we couldn't grind it."

Juno hastened to the kitchen and returned with what food there was cooked. Edward, holding to his mother's skirt, pointed to the heavy boots: "It's dem what make de tracks. Law, dey will neber wear dose shoes out till kingdom come."

13

"Will you give us a few dry peas?" the men asked, after having devoured bits of hard, saltless cornbread.

With a questioning look at me Dick hurried off, returning with his hat full.

A few fell to the ground. The soldiers picked them up, showing thus their early training in thrift. But Dick, prodigal of his master's provisions, offered to bring more.

"Thanks, lady ; these are enough. We've been round a good ways since Sherman started for the sea, and now know why our prisoners aren't better fed. No one can blame a government for feeding their wives and children first. Lady, if you could see my wife and beautiful little girl in Michigan, you wouldn't wonder I'm longing to get to them before I die." And the sick man wept aloud.

At first Lydia's countenance showed that she was indignant; she was recalling to mind our hours of recent anxiety. But the tears of a man, and he a soldier, softened her. "Boss," said she, her voice having a ring of tenderness, "boss, why don't you go home ter your wife an' daughter; if I was you I wouldn't stay a day fightin' us."

My husband, who had returned the night before, at that moment reined in his pony at the gate. He lifted from his eyes the blue shade. What! Bluecoats at his very door, surrounded by his wife and servants!

"What does this mean? What's your business here?" he demanded.

The soldier replied, "My friend is ill. On the march from Tomshear we were obliged to rest in the wood, and so have strayed from our corps and been without bread for a week till this good lady (pointing to Juno) gave us a hoecake. We've tried, but couldn't find a ford to these nasty creeks."

Revilo knew that they were deserters. "Up! march!" he said; "I'll show you a ford. Your corps are encamped near Hatfield. I'll see you safely there. There is no prison nearer than Tomshear, or you'd not have your liberty."

Dick forgot to lead away the pony, he was so interested in the soldiers.

Revilo jumped into his saddle and accompanied the two men through the pine-land trail, on to the turnpike. They were out of sight ere it dawned upon me the danger of his going off unarmed with two of our enemies. By my command, Dick, on a bareback mule, hastened to the fields for Belfast and his men to go at once to their master's assistance.

Lydia tried to console me: "No man what

talks so good 'bout his wife an' child'll harm our master. I do wish dose blue-coats had neber come south. We was all livin' peaceful an' happy, wid plenty ter eat, salt as cheap as dirt. Now, clothes is scarce; even de foreman treads barefoot. Next t'ing massa an' missy'll have ter do de same: dey livin' ter-day in a log-pen not fit fer a poor 'cracker.' I wonder if Bro' Molbro is got any shoes? Amos sent word by Mars Gus' ole man Pete dat in Faginia daid soldiers, grey an' blue, is lyin' round not more dan a foot under ground. Jackals an' wolfs has good pickin' o' nights. He say on eb'ry side is big cannons ready fer a bomb match ter belch out red-hot balls. De war has only brought sorrow an' tribilation. I'll be glad when we kin go ter Swansea. If we beautiful w'ite house is burned down massa kin build anodder."

A few weeks after, we learned that Green Forest was occupied by a Federal regiment, twelve hundred strong. The general commanded his men to pitch their tents, the driving of pins and the flapping of canvas making great confusion.

Inanimate nature could express no feeling, else the grey moss, dragged from the trees for soldier's bedding, would have bristled into needles, and the fire, made of fences, sent forth snakes to poison the soldiers' food.

At the family home, at this time, was Chim, with her son, whose father, a major, was stationed at Vicksburg; Letha and her baby, Lalla a bride; Flossie, a girl of thirteen; and Sonnie, Nannie's foster-child.

During the war, girls would marry, although their young husbands shouldered guns after the ceremony, and returned to camp-life.

The general with his staff had the house ransacked, hoping to find Confederate soldiers.

Women and children were forced into one chamber, while the officers settled themselves in the others, making the dining-room their mess-hall, the parlour their headquarters. The growth of months in the kitchen-garden was consumed in one hour. The negroes, too, returning from the fields, found their coops empty, and every mouthful of food in their cabins gone.

For protection, black children huddled round Granny, who stood in a doorway, her arms akimbo; not daring to express her thought—" What business has you blue-coats on we Green Forest ? "

A soldier seized one piccaninny by his shirt, on the point of a bayonet, his legs, arms, and head meeting, while he yelled lustily for help.

The storeroom likewise was emptied of the little it contained. Affie, old and feeble, hobbling on sticks, remonstrated. "Boss," she pleaded, "you what is all civered with gold, is you willin' ter see ole massa's chilluns starve? We w'ite mens wouldn't do dat way, caise massa always tell de niggars ter treat omens well. Law, what would he say if he could lift he head from Midway graveyard ! "

They laughed at her naïve speech.

Affie consulted with Hetty and Nanny as to the best way to feed the inmates of that rear room. " My Jack couldn't sleep last night," said she, "he was groanin' de best part o' de time. I's a man, Affie, if my face is black; how kin we git we w'ite folks out o' dis glomeration, if only ter Riseburg ? '

"' Riseburg! Why Jack, Uncle Scipio say you can't see de co't house de place is plump full o' gol' buttons an' shinin' swords stickin' in de gun mouth. We guns ain't like dat. I asked yister-day if I could give de baby some mush, de soldier jes' level dat p'int at my t'roat an' I feel my palate cut clean out. We ain't used ter sech suf-fusion. What is we ter do ? "

Each night the old lunch box—made for mid-day luncheons—was smuggled through the win-dow, the most of its contents begged from the soldiers, by negro women.

After the burning of the gin-house and other

buildings, Chim implored the general to send them under flag of truce to the Confederate lines.

He gladly consented.

Accordingly, at midnight, a two-wheeled cart drove to the gate for the party of seven.

One trunk only was allowed. With tears in her eyes Lalla turned over and over her scant bridal attire, trying to decide what to take, what to leave. A chill in the night air enabled them to double their garments, greatly impeding their gait. Hoopskirts being still in fashion, from horizontal white-oak splits dangled bunches of silver spoons, forks, and a cream jug.

When Flossie appeared, a Yankee officer asked: "Where has this beautiful girl been? I searched this house myself, yet never saw her."

Very likely! Under a high poster valanced bed, Nannie had spread a pallet, where the fair blonde had spent her days. Guarded by Jack, Frank, or Scipio, she exercised after tattoo.

In leaving, Nannie forgot her fear of the officer; so grasping her foster-son's hand, she said, "Boss, dis is my ole missus' las' baby, she died w'en he was only a few hours old; I's suckled de blessed child. Oh! mister, don't let no harm come ter him! He's powerful high-tempered, but w'en I says, 'Sonnie, who trouble you?' he t'rows he arms round my neck, so,"—embracing the frightened boy, causing even Yankee eyes to blur.

The lad was kindly treated.

On the Sandy Run road, a mile from Green Forest, Jack and two others awaited the cart, bringing corn hoe-cakes, and hoping to go with the refugees. Denied this, they bade the fleeing party good-bye. "Take care of yourself, ma'am," Frank enjoined, " come back soon ! We'll do we best at Green Forest ; but it ain't home widout we w'ite folks. We wish we had some meat for you."

Noting Letha's feeble condition, the sergeant in charge assisted her to mount the horse's back, her feet resting upon the shaft. From one side to another she wriggled, but eventually begged the driver to allow her to dismount. "Your horse's bones are sharp," she said, " I'd rather walk." In fact, she was seated on an unseen solid silver cream-jug.

Beyond the white flag, trials were not yet at end ; for food was scarce, and famine tugged at the vitals of every one within the Confederate lines. The officers shared their scanty store with the women, then sent them under escort toward Tomshear. They hoped to reach Pine Knot, where a welcome would be theirs, if not food.

The lowlands were now inundated. This

compelled the women to remove their only pair of shoes and stockings, and wade for hours in mud and slush. Eventually, footsore and weary, they halted in a deserted village, to rest for a day or so. The cabbage-palmetto, wild berries, and a few pounds of corn meal bought on the journey, constituted their food.

Letha and the Confederate sergeant pushed on, hoping to secure provisions from a commissary in charge of a train, reported to be near Blackheath. They secured all that they could carry, but decided to stay one night, to be ready for an early start.

Before dawn the villagers were roused by the cry, " Yankees, Yankees ! "

Sergeant Way jumped out of his bedroom window, knowing his fate if captured wearing the grey. The little place was completely surrounded, and, despite Letha's entreaties and her assurances that he was only conducting her to a place of safety, he was taken prisoner, and bound.

Unable to lift his hat, he cheerily called from the captured train : Don't trouble about me ; I'm truly sorry you've lost that fine side of bacon."

Lieutenant Mills hearing of his bride's flight, received a furlough to pursue her. He found her in Blackheath with her sisters. Their camping outfit comprised one tin boiler, a wooden bucket, two plates, and three cups, with dozens of spoons and other solid silverware.

Bravely they now set out on the long journey to Pine Knot, where, in fact, there was a spirit of keen unrest ; for wild rumours of the fall of Saver-nake and other important places made us uneasy.

That mysterious, intangible post-bag—planta-tion-gossip, with never a letter—had brought to Lydia news of Flora's sudden death. She strove to master her excitement, but failed. At her dic-tation, I wrote Marlborough a letter on a square of wall paper, ending with a Scripture text: "Bro' Molbro, don't forgit Mars C. C.'s words, 'Keep your heart full o' de love o' God, an' so live in peace an' everlastin' rest."

This letter never reached him. Amos and he were on the road to Green Forest, with the body of their master, Captain Fleming Janes, his sword forever sheathed.

This sad news had not reached Pine Knot. Indeed, instead of mourning, we were rejoicing over a gift of sausages, spare-ribs, and chine-bones sent by Revilo's father, who held the post of commissary in Savernake. These trimmings were a part of his pay. One evening we had just finished a greasy, saltless supper, and were sitting in the open hallway, wondering why news came neither from Virginia nor Siberty County.   Lydia was cuddling " her boy " to sleep, when the rumble of wheels and a helloa at the gate startled us.

" Who is there ?   What do you wish ? " Revilo called.

A strange voice replied, " Weary travellers."

Men having been called to the gate, and shot down in cold blood, I clung to Revilo, imploring him not to go until Dick could bring a light-wood torch.   But he went, I holding to his coat-tail. We reached the gate before Dick.

A disguised voice asked : " Can you shelter us for the night ? "   Revilo replied, " We have only two rooms and one bed."

" We are so tired ! and the women fainting with hunger.   Do let us sleep on the floor."

A child's cry for a bit of bread touched the tenderest chord of our hearts, and we unhesitatingly replied : " Come in, and be welcome.   We will share what we have."

A trembling female voice said : " Thank you very much, we are hungry and tired."   The light from Dick's torch just then shone into the travellers' faces—they were my own sisters, driven by Lalla's young husband.

Like wildfire this news spread.   Our negro cabins were accordingly soon empty, the negroes flocking to greet " old massa's chilluns."

" Whey is you come from, missy : How is de folks at Green Forest ? Law! how tired dey look. 'Pon my soul, dey is hongry. Honey, does you want a piece o' bread ? Ain't you eat a mouthful ter-day ? "

Juno and others bustled about the kitchen, preparing another supper, while Lydia knelt beside Chim, her head on the nurse's shoulder. Stroking her soft white hands, Lydia was too overpowered with grief and joy to ask a single question.

On the floor Letha lay, full length, her dark ringlets scattered over Clarinda's lap, while black fingers passed over and over her weary brow. The nervous tension was relaxed upon reaching this haven of rest.

Our pine table was soon spread ; with a platter of smoking sausages and corn hoe-cakes—the entire bill of fare. Into those hungry eyes there came a look one sees in Zoological gardens at the feeding hour.

Unbidden, the negro women stripped corn shucks into shreds, and converted the cloth from the loom into a covering for a mattress, thus making the travellers comfortable.

XVI.

"Is this post day?"

" Sweet are the uses of adversity,
  Which, like the toad, ugly and venomous,
  Wears yet a precious jewel in his head."
                                        SHAKESPEARE.

DEFEAT seemed imminent, yet hope buoyed us up; we believed that the sun of victory would soon arise.   Even as stars are hidden behind clouds, so we insisted that from beneath a canopy of discouragements, rejoicing might yet ride forth.

All over the land widows were blending their wails with the mourns of mothers and sisters.

At Pine Knot we were cut off from the world as completely as if living at the antipodes. Although Abraham Lincoln promulgated the Emancipation, January 1, 1863, we had not heard of it.   The papers that reached us were mostly out of date, and filled with names of the killed and wounded.   True we had heard of the sinking of the Alabama by the Kearsarge, and that her men with calmness awaited their doom, losing their ship, but not their honour; of "our boys in grey" subsisting on half-rations, marching on shoeless feet, unyielding till every man was prostrate in the trenches. General Lee, we felt sure, would lower his flag to none other in the land.

The tattered uniforms and hob-nailed boots of officers that once sat in law offices, professors' chairs, or on plantation piazzas told a tale of heroism as clearly as did the words of a Federal Colonel at Gettysburg when he called to his men, saying, "Boys, don't shoot; it's a pity to kill such brave fellows."

About our cabin scorched wire-grass showed, here and there fresh green blades sparkling with dew. Mocking-birds, thrush, blue-jays, and logger-heads sang in chorus as only birds can sing. The glow of a spring day was as serene as if the universe were one vast brotherhood at peace. My morning was engrossed with the care of sick negroes, and on returning home, Revilo's whistle sounded. I hastened to the gate in time to welcome him. He dismounted, with a newspaper in hand.

"Is this post day?" I asked.

Not a word did he reply; his cheeks were pale as death, his lips set tight.

"Are you ill?" I continued. National adversity was obliterated by the fear of family trouble.

In those wild days women learned not to multiply words, scarcely to shed a tear. With Revilo hand in hand, I entered the cabin. Dick stabled the pony: it was white with foam.

A hapless future must have mapped itself out to cause Revilo such emotion ; he was usually calm and self-contained.

With a heave of his breast, he slowly struggled to articulate the words: "The war is ended; General Lee is defeated,—not conquered. Our slaves are free. Dare I tell you that we are impoverished? Oh, have I lived to meet this hour?"

"Yes," I answered, "and we will stem the tide of adversity. Remember, your life is spared, while thousands have been killed by bullets. Don't trouble about your wife; for true love smooths the roughest way, even if it doesn't make the pot boil."

A smile suffused his face. The look of despair was supplanted by one of resolve. Lifting his eyes, he said, "God helping me, with energy and industry I will yet surmount this trial."

On that rough-hewn log floor, we, husband and wife, knelt, each offering a silent petition.

This shock to us was like unto that felt by a

ship's crew wrecked in mid-ocean ; there was no gleam of hope from even a distant shore ; our minds were stunned by the fact of our poverty. The mere abolition of slavery gave us little concern in that hour—our thoughts were engrossed with the certainty of want and starvation. The future gnashed its teeth, making it almost mockery for us to hope.

Only time could convince of the ultimate good to both parties.

Taking the dinner-bugle down, Revilo sounded three long blasts.

Our labourers came from the fields, Belfast inquiring if the work was to be changed?

" No. Congregate at the front in an hour's time. I have something to say to you."

Groups of men and women soon were seen talking, their quick-drawn breath betraying their anxiety. " What has happened that we must leave off work when grass is overrunning cotton an' corn ? Has anyone been stealin' ? "

Overhead the sun was just past the meridian.

The next day it would arise on a new existence for the black man ; for his brow was about to be crowned with the cap of freedom. It may be interesting, even at this late day, to listen to the negroes' welcome to freedom. Personal expe-

rience only is given, save that of a friend that
happened to be in Augusta, and inquired of an
old negro-woman what was the unusual noise in
the next street. " Law, missy, ain't you heard
de news ? Mars Sherman is arriv'd ; he sen' a wud
round dat de Lord is gib ter de Et'opian de wings
o' de mornin' an' tell dem ter flee ter de utmost
part o' de earth. An' dey is a gwine. Is you
want ter buy any berries ter-day, dey is cheap an'
sweet, honey ? "

But to return. As requested, our negroes gathered about the steps, the men removing their
wire-grass hats, the women dropping a low courtesy. The scene was not picturesque as of yore ;
instead of gay bandannas, bits of faded cloth
bound the women's heads. Lydia sat on the step
with " her boy " on her knee ; she realised something unusual had happened. Of its significance
she was as ignorant as those that lived in the
quarters.

With undisguised agitation my husband rose
from his rudely-constructed bench and unfolded
a square of wall paper, received that morning at
the post office.

" This newspaper," said he,—for such it was,—
" brings to us important news. I want each one
to listen attentively, then try to show by your
conduct that you are sensible men and women.

14

You know for four years there has been hard
fighting between the Yankees and we of the south.
You have heard the cannon, and this many a
month have suffered for food and clothing. Our
beloved General Lee has been for a time surrounded by a vast army, and now, with his men starving in the trenches, he has been forced to lay
down his sword before the Yankee General, Grant.
For months I myself have realised that our men
could not fight much longer with empty knapsacks
and canteens. A proclamation made by Abe
Lincoln then comes into force."—He stopped,
scarcely able to articulate.—"This changes all
of you from slaves into free men and women.
Many of you were born slaves of our parents.
God knows we, their children, have tried to do our
duty to you. Your young mistress has nursed
you on cold winter nights when death seemed
hovering over you."

"Dat she has, massa! You both on you has!
God knows you's been good ter us, an' He's writ
it in de big book!" said old Sawney, his words
indicating that, with encouragement, he would
shout " Glory, hallelujah ! "

My husband's voice still trembled. " Remember, freedom does not mean a pocketful of money,
with plenty to eat and wear ! You are really
homeless, and now must feed and clothe your-

selves and your children. Confederate money is
of no more value than waste paper,"—taking from
his pocket a roll of one-hundred dollar bills.

Following his example, negro men turned
over the paper currency in their possession, not
grasping the fact of its utter worthlessness. They
rammed the bills down into their trouser-pockets,
resolving to spend them that very night at the
country store, where occasionally they bought a
twist of tobacco or a pound of sugar.

" There must be a tremendous change over the
whole country," Revilo continued, "and much
suffering, before matters adjust themselves. You
know I am renting this plantation. The mules,
the wagons, and farming utensils are all mine.
Not an ax or hoe do you own; nor a stick of
wood to make a fire in your cabins!—which also
belong to me. You haven't a foot of land where-
on to plant corn or cotton; you have not yet received the mule and forty acres promised with
freedom. I doubt if you ever get it."

Sawney murmured: " I told hunno people it
was a black lie."

" I haven't had time to think of the best plan,"
Revilo went on to say, " but one thing I do know,
the crops you have planted must die without your
care. If you work on as usual, until Christmas,
I will divide everything into three parts: one

part must pay the rent and feed the stock; another pay for provisions and clothing, which I must advance for you and your children, defraying also my family expenses. At the end of harvest the third part will be divided equally between you ; thus giving you something to live on until you can find employment. For, owing to my failing sight, I must go where there is a doctor.

"Try, then, not to let this new order of things turn your heads. Remember it is no disgrace to be under my authority. Each of us must obey some one ; my wife here, as you know, rules me." He thus gave a cheerful turn to his words, noticing how overwhelmed I was.

His brother, one arm in a sling,—wounded by a bayonet thrust,—then rose and read the proclamation aloud.

Each word fell upon my ear with a heavy stroke ; but in the midst of my despair joy filled my heart. Revilo was overpowered by the effort he had made, yet beneath his shaded brow was an expression of perfect peace. It told how truly he had tried to be a humane master.

He rose, and, as a father talking to children, again addressed the negroes, who still stood with heads uncovered, their eyes and mouths wide open, their faces a study in surprise, amazement, and incredulity.

"Do you understand what my brother has read?"

The foreman Belfast touched his forehead: "Massa, it sounds bery strange, but fer my part me an' mine is going ter stay here jes as we is. Odder folks kin do as dey choose, I knows when I's well off." Turning to the crowd of negroes, he said : "Hunno people, you has permission now fer speak your mind."

The frightened look on many faces gave place to expressions of joy. "Don't be troubled, massa," one cried, "we none of us wants ter leave you an' missy."

Another asked : "Whey's we ter go? Who's ter feed us? We has no money, we has no land, no mule, no house. Lord! what is we ter do? We don't want any odder master. He might beat us."

Sawney, at Pine Knot, like Frank at Green Forest, was the watchman over the spiritual interest of the people. Deeming it now his privilege to speak, he advanced close beside the cabin step, his grey hairs shining in the sunlight. Bowing to his master, he crossed his thin hands over his breast.

"Hunno people," said he, "Mars C. C. read 'bout how de Lord had no place fer lay He head; not so much as de foxes or de birds of de air. I's a t'inkin' we is jes de same. Some on us is gettin' ole an' can't work much longer. Sometime we'll be sick, sometime we must die. Wid no massa, wid no missy, law, what trouble dey is ter be, sech tribilation we has neber t'ought o' yit. Some on you may fly off ter git your forty acres an' mule. Hear me, it's a lie! Afore you knows, you'll be beggin' or stealin', caise ole massa say dey is only three ways ter make a livin'. I tends ter work long as I kin lift a hoe right here wid we good massa."

His earnestness had its effect. The breathless stillness of that eventful day was broken by a chorus of voices : "You is say de true word, Uncle Sawney, we has no 'tention ter leave we w'ite folks."

Lydia and "her boy" were in a tight embrace. The child wondered at his dear nurse's tears ; they recalled to him the death and burial of little Lydia, an infant of Belfast, who had been recently laid beneath the pines.

"Mommer, don't cry," he begged, his wee white hand brushing her tears away. "Don't cry, I love you so much. Who's dead, mommer?"

Through my own tears I saw drops falling over my husband's full beard. We had long dreaded the culmination of an unequal strife between Yankees and Southerners, yet when the end did come, it stunned us. Certainly we had not dreamed of having such proofs of love and devotion from our coloured people, who were now suddenly elevated to the platform of freedom. The turning loose of these millions was as if an orphan school were disbanded, with the words: " Children, go into the world ; provide you homes, food and clothing ; the land is rich with gold and silver ; dig and coin money for yourselves.

With no experience, building material, or food ; without a spade with which to dig, how could they make a living? True, Lincoln split rails, and Franklin set up type ; but some one ordered the number of rails, and written pages were furnished Franklin.

Mere work does not ensure a full meal or a couch on which to rest. Our former slaves were unlettered, and wholly unused to take thought for the morrow. Freedom then dawned to many not so much with gladness, as with a dread of the unborn future.

In very truth the flag of the Shenandoah had now dipped, never more to wave from flag-staff or mast-head.

Marlborough and Amos had, but a few weeks before, returned with their master's body. In Midway they laid him to rest, the grey moss waving like a flag of peace over his grave.

Marlborough then hastened to Professor Lamont's plantation.   His wife had died a month
before, leaving her children in care of her blind
father.

Marlborough realised now that he had his
family to support.   And he with not a shingle to
cover their heads, and only a roll of worthless Confederate paper-money in his pockets!

Flora's master again took the chair of a pro-
fessorship, giving little thought to his estate in
Siberty County.   It remained in possession of
his former slaves.

Marlborough, not knowing what to do with
his family, quite naturally turned to Lydia for
comfort and advice.

By word of mouth,—the negro's only means
of communication,—she heard that her friend and
old lover would soon be with her, hoping to find
employment in the neighbourhood.

This news aroused in Robin a keen dread lest
he should lose a good wife and a mother for his
children ; for free negroes might not think slave-
marriages binding.   " Dat rascal, what broke my
leg an' cut my t'roat, is got no wife now.   He's
comin' here ter steal my Lyddy.   Folks says love
is always young.   I myself is seed w'ite folks
marry wid one foot in de grave, but I'll show dat
fellow dat I's a free man an' kin come an' go as I

chooses." Shaking off the lethargy his well-kept cabin had superinduced, he informed Lydia of his intention of going to Tomshear after the crops were divided ; there, she could take in washing and ironing ; ladies might do a bit of housework, but shirt-fronts they couldn't iron !

Lydia made no secret of her delight at the prospect of greeting Marlborough. He had come home, she said, " a live soldier, wid a cockade of vict'ry in he hat." The dagger she had dreaded, she now spoke of as lying on a battle-field, where she knew Marlborough had more than once drawn it in defence of his master. In her imaginative mind these onesided battles were fought over and over with never a defeat where her loved ones were engaged.

After his return Amos lost no time ; he married his girl. But up to a moment before the ceremony she was grumbling because she hadn't one inch of white tarlatan for a veil, nor a pair of old white gloves to cover her black hands : " I ain't no more dan half a bride," she pouted, "in such no 'count clo's." She gave her frock a spiteful toss.

Her husband was more fortunate ; he wore his master's military coat with epaulettes, brass buttons, and gold braid, looking every inch a man any girl might be proud to marry. A red cockade, too, of a Federal trooper's, which he had picked up after a battle, in Virginia, he now stuck in his hat.

No one was prouder than he of his experience at the front. Siberty County negroes listened to his blood-curdling accounts of hair-breadth escapes, feeling that supernatural spirits must have guarded him.

For all time Amos was a personage.

XVII.

Lydia's Ghost Story.

"I sing the hymn of the conquered who fell in the battle of life,
  The hymn of the wounded, the beaten, who died overwhelmed
    in the strife;
  The hymn of the low and the humble, the weary, the broken in
    heart,
Who strove and who failed."

W. W. STORY.

THE life of every one forced to bend his will to that of another, must be beset with trying hours and bitter hardships.

So, too, Lydia's life had not been all sunshine; but she had prized her joys and cherished the flowers that bloomed in her pathway.

Therefore, when the day came that she was freed from all shackles of slavery—quitting the room adjoining the one metaphorically occupied, as it had been, by "Uncle Tom" and his chains—we hear wailing rather than rejoicing.

The following poem is so characteristic of the way Lydia felt, and also the way she expressed herself regarding her freedom, I venture to insert

it. The author I do not know, and I cannot
vouch for the authenticity of the dialect :

> "Oh, mammy, have you heard the news ? "
> Thus spoke a Southern child,
> As in the nurse's aged face,
> She upward glanced and smiled.

> " What news you mean, my little one ?
> It must be mighty fine,
> To make my darling's face so red,
> Her sunny blue eyes shine ! "

> " Why Abram Lincoln, don't you know,
> The Yankee President,
> Whose ugly picture once we saw
> When up to town we went ;

> " Why, he is going to free you all,
> And make you rich and grand,
> And you'll be dressed in silk and gold,
> Like the proudest in the land.

> " A gilded coach shall carry you
> Where'er you wish to ride,
> And, mammy, all your work shall be
> Forever laid aside."

> The eager speaker paused for breath,
> And then the old nurse said,
> While closer to her swarthy cheek
> She pressed the golden head,

"My little missus, stop an' res',
  You's talkin' mighty fas',
Jes' look up dere an' tell me what
  You see in yonder glass.

"You see ole mammy's wrinkled face,
  As black as any coal,
An' underneath her handkerchief
  Whole heaps of knotty wool.

"My darlin's face is red an' white,
  Her skin is sof' an' fine,
An' on her prutty little head
  De yaller ringlets shine.

"My chile, who made dis difference
  'Twixt mammy an' 'twixt you?
You reads it in de dear Lord's book,
  An' you kin tell me true.

"De dear Lord said it must be so,
  An', honey, I for one
Wid t'ankful heart will always say
  His holy will be done.

"I t'anks Mars Lunkin, all de same,
  But when I wants for free
I'll ask de Lord ob glory,—
  Not poor buckra man, like he.

"An' as for gilded carriages
  Dey's berry fine to see,
But massa's coach what carries him
  Is good enough for me.

" An', honey, when your mammy wants
    To change her homespun dress,
She'll pray, like dear ole missus,
    To be clothed with righteousness.

" My work's been done dis many a day,
    An' now I takes my ease ;
A-waitin' for de Master's call
    Jes' when de Master please.

" And when at last de time done come
    An' poor ole granny dies,
Your own dear mother's sof' white han'
    Shall close dese tired old eyes.

" De dear Lord Jesus soon will take
    Ole mammy home to Him,
An' He can wash my guilty soul
    From eb'ry stain of sin.

" An' at his feet I shall lie down
    Who died an' rose for me,
An' den, an' not till den, my chile,
    Your mammy shall be free.

" Come, little missus, say your prayers,
    Let ole Mars Lunkin 'lone,
De Lord knows who b'longs to him
    An' he'll care for his own."

Lydia, in tears, told how " De folk at de quarters was talkin' 'bout goin' ter live at Green Forest ag'in ; dey t'inks dey'll be happy deir ; but dey'll find it ain't home widout de w'ite chilluns. Bro' Robin kin go wid his family ; I sha'n't leave my boy fer any o' dem. Miss Dodo," she said, turning to me, "is it right fer Bro' Robin ter drag me away? Bro' Molbro wouldn't 'fuse me dis joy. Now I's gittin grey"—lifting the border of a new bandanna that " her boy " had given her.

The child threw himself into her arms. " You sha'n't go, mommer. Daddy Robin can't take you away. I'm hugging you. I'll be a man when my pants are finished ; then you can live with me."

" Oh, my sweet chile, I won't go. No, I won't go fer no free nigger, if he is my husband. Colonel Ross is talkin' nonsense at de politic meetens he's holdin' at Mars Bob's plantation. 'You niggars is fools,' says he. Some fine mornin' you'll wake up slaves ag'in. Four years I fought ter set you free; why don't you come an' plant cotton fer me? In dozens of New York banks I've piles of greenbacks. My wife an' daughter dress better dan anyone in de settlement, an' if your w'ite folks were kindhearted dey'd call."

Allured by Colonel Ross's offer, Daniel asked permission to leave us ; he gave as his reason his engagement to the colonel's cook.

His happiness, however, was short-lived. The

black queen of the pots and skillets tossed him
aside in a few weeks for " one more suited ter her
understandin' as cook ter a rich buckra man
whose coat was civered wid gold, two golden tip-
pets on he shoulders an' a red rooster's tail wavin'
in he hat,"

Daniel married Judy, his old love.

Lydia told again how "Colonel Ross had said,
'thousands of Yankees was rottin' in deir graves
ter give dem freedom.'

"What does I care if dey is?" she said. "We
neber 'vited dem ter leave deir wives an' daughters
ter be killed.   I knows one t'ing; if it hadn't been
fer free niggars, ter-day I'd be Mrs. Molbro Janes,
wid de best husban' dat ever lived.

"Ah, missy," she continued, " soon we's all ter
be scattered ; Juno an' Dick is goin' ter ole Jim.
He say he must see Boy an' Cissy a-fore he
dies."

Lydia wished to name her first grandchild
" Molbro," but Juno the mother thought it
ought to be Dick or Marmaduke. Dick, the
father, however, declared it should be neither,
but Jim, after *his* " pa."   Before the infant was
named, it received the nickname " Boy," which was
entered in our plantation book.

Although I longed to retain Lydia in our service, yet it seemed unwise to interfere. We had

never broken family ties in slavery days; why
should we break them now?

Lydia strove day by day to cheer and enliven
our home, knowing that to us the future appeared
dark. A bright smile wreathed her black face
when she opened our cabin-door, seemingly for-
getful of troubles that pricked her own heart. In
the spirit of the olden days she recalled many
amusing occurrences that had happened in the
nursery at Green Forest. A ghost story well
known to us her older "w'ite chilluns" she re-
lated now to "her boy," with enthusiasm.

"Ober at Mars Ben's," said she, "dey was a
man called Sambo, whose wife lived a mile t'other
side Midway cem't'ry. Sambo went ter his wife's
house 'fore dark, but one night he was belated,
an' when beside de wall a col' breeze blowed in
he face and icy fingers gripped he ear-tips.
Standin' a few yards off was a life-size ghos' in
long wavin' hair an' w'ite robes. Sambo first
t'ought he'd scream, den he 'membered no one
lived near by, so he held he breaf les' he might
wake up odder daid people. He wound he arms
round a saplin', an' he never could tell how he an'
dat tree parted comp'ny. When he come ter he
senses his wife Mary was settin' bolt upright in
bed screamin', 'Sambo is you plum 'stracted? Is
dis de way fer come in a decent 'oman's house?

11

Git along wid you ! Don't hug me till you learns
'spectful manners.' "

" ' Mary, Mary,' he cried, ' is a sperit come in
de dooe behin' me ? It had my ear-tips tight
'twixt its cold, bony fingers. ' Sambo by dis
time was under de blankets, wid shoes an' hat.
In de corn fields nex' day de folks neber give
de poor feller any res.' All he say was, ' If any
you mens want ter go ter Mary's cabin a'ter dark,
go 'long wid you. If massa don't 'low me time
by daylight it's a long week 'fore Sambo's visage
'll 'luminate de portal of dat house ober at Mars
Abel's. ' In Siberty County even de w'ite folks
didn't like ter pass de graveyard. A chu'ch
meetin' was called an' de elders 'structed Sambo's
boss ter send him on a Monday night ter show
dem where de ghos' could be seen. ' Massa,'
says he, ' I likes fer 'bey w'ite folks, but, believe
me, sah, nobody'll git me in gunshot o' dat brick
wall a'ter dark. ' Deacon Quarterly promised
him a new beaver hat an' Sunday go-ter-meeten
clothes, so he 'greed ter meet dem at de cross
roads if dey would bring a horse fer him ter ride.
He didn't have no peace ; de men 'lowed he'd
break an' run at de fust sight o' de chu'ch steeple.

" ' Bro' Gus, ' said Sambo, ' don't you put bad
mouth on me, my old beaver is done gone ter
pieces. Don't you t'ink mens what prays 'loud

in chu'ch kin keep off ghos'? I may clim' a tree, but folks say if a ghos' teches a saplin' even a 'possum can't hold on.'

"De men jogged 'long, one star af'er annoder twinklin' over head. Bullfrogs was croakin' an' katydid an' katydidn'ts quar'ling. Pres'n'ly, Bro' Sambo jerked up he horse. 'Massa, we better hitch here, caise when a horse feels a cold win' deir hair rises, an' wid backin' deir ears, no man kin keep de saddle. It's de hones' truf, sah, dat's how Jack loss he fron' teeth.' He young massa had com' home a sure 'nough doctor, and 'lowed he mus' have grave-yard bones ter study de corp'ration of de niggar. He bribe Bro' Jack ter help him. Dey had bust open de coffin an' shove de daid niggar in de cart when a cold win' blowed about deir ears. Mars Dr. Sam call out, 'Jack, pick up dose lines an' drive fer your life.' Bro' Jack no sooner stoop dan de ole blin' mare, what's gentle as a lam', let fly her heels an' plum' square hit dem front teeth. Mars Dr. Sam pitch dat fellow in de cart, an' he neber knowed 'till de got ter de stable but what he had two daid nig- gars ter hide. Folks was dumfounded when Bro' Jack com' ter work wid no teeth. It was six months 'fore dey hear how dey was pulled.

"Midway's old clock was strikin' 'leven when de mens tied deir horses. Deacon Quarterly handed

Sambo a cigar. 'T'ank you, massa,' he said, 'ter-
morrow I'll smoke. Sperits don't like brimstone,
matches, or 'bacca. Law, massa, I has goose-
flesh a crawlin' down my back. Does you feel
creepy? By jolly! dar he is! dar!' pointing in
de direction of de stone wall. He neber bet'ought
him 'bout de pony, but ran eb'ry step of de way
ter Mary's cabin. De w'ite mens seein' a sure-
'nough w'ite figger wid flowin' robes, los' no time,
but mounted deir saddles. Dey was so scared dey
neber stopped ter look fer deir own horses. Folks
neber knowd how does beasts got in de wrong
stables. One pony stomped 'long side de tree all
night, neighin' in de mornin' fer he feed. Mary's
husband got he beaver an' Sunday clothes. Folks
say afterward it was two young mens home from
college what found where de ghos' hid heself.
Watchin' one night, dey followed plum' ter Widder Cook's, an' saw de sperit wid no key turn de
front door-lock; an' if it didn't walk straight ter
de widder's bed an' lie 'long side de poor w'ite
lady what folks say was weepin' fer her husband
who had jes been buried in Midway grave-yard."
(Rich Mrs. Cook, it seems, walked in her sleep.)

Lydia told " her boy " this long ghostly narration with as much earnestness as if it had happened but the week before.

The first months of that eventful year of 1865,

and of freedom, wore on apace. Corn-shucks turned brown and sear. Busy squirrels darted from tree to tree in search of pine-mast for their winter store. In this they were better off than many of us, having a goodly supply; we had only a handful of food.

Sawney and his wife, both old and feeble, gave us no end of anxiety. Sawney fell ill. Business calling us to Halby, we stopped at the old man's cabin to give directions about his medicines.

"Don't stay long, missy," he pleaded, "Sawney is hoe he las' row. I's nearin' de end, ma'am. I feels pow'rful weak an' is prayin' de same word me an' my old 'oman pray when massa tell 'bout Mars Abe Linkin. I says dat day, 'Ole 'oman, is you got it in yer head dat massa is a free man? Sure as you an' me is borned he ain't bleeged ter stay here tarrifyin' he soul an' body feedin' us; he's a free man. We kneel down an' den I lifts my voice ter de Fadder's throne. 'O Lord,' says I, 'if it is dy holy will, let we missy close we eye; let me an' de ole 'oman lie under de pines wid de baby Liddy till de trumphet calls we dry bones ter de ressarection cou't!' Don't stay long, ma'am, caise de year'll soon term'nate. What's me an' Clarinder ter do?"

"At five on Friday," I said, "we will be home. Don't trouble about your future. God has promised to have a care of those who trust Him. Take your gruel regularly."

"De Lord's will be done. Good-bye, little massa. How is de pet lam'?"

The child answered cheerily, "Mommer's goin' to feed it. I'll bring it to see you when we get home."

A sandy road retarded our return, but, nearing the cabins, Dick urged his mules, excited as he was by seeing a crowd in front of Sawney's cabin. Turning to me he said, "Dey's somet'ing happen, ma'am; look at de folks ober yonder."

The negroes cried, "Come, missy, come, de old man's ben a-callin' fer you dis half hour; de charyot is swing low; he's a-prayin' fer it ter stan' still, jes ter de hour when massa an' missy come. It's a-waitin' fer you, ma'am!"

Sawney's glazed eyes turned toward us as we opened the cabin-door, his emaciated hands reaching for an invisible object. "Is dat de charyot wheels a-rumblin'?" he asked. "Yes, Lord, here is me. On de strike o' de five missy say she'll be home. Deir, I feels her sof' han'. Shut my eye, ma'am; I's lay down de shovel an' de hoe. Lord, here is me! Amen!"

So Sawney died. And we all believed that the Christmas-tide found him in the keeping of His Saviour, a ransomed soul.

One night a month after, the fire burning low, Phoebe his daughter, with a new-born infant sleeping in her arms, complained of being cold. Clarinder hastened in search of wood, when a downpour of rain saturated her garments, and she took cold, developing pleurisy. Without a flicker, as with one puff of wind, her life was extinguished. Providence, fate, or whatever one chooses to call the power that decides our future, provided for this aged couple.

My husband and I, attended by the plantation negroes, followed her plain deal coffin. Under the pines we buried her, the old plantation song of " Uncle Ned " ringing in our minds.

XVIII.

Valentine Versus April-fool.

"Why shadow the beauty of sea or of land
        With a doubt or a fear ?
God holds all the swift-rolling worlds in His hand
And sees what no man can as yet understand,
        That out of life here,
        With its smile and its tear,
Comes forth into light, from Eternity planned,
        The soul of good cheer.'
            Don't worry—
        The end shall appear.
                ELIZABETH PORTER GOULD.

AFTER the produce of the place was gar-
nered, the bugle summoned the negroes
for a division.

"Whey is you goin', massa ? " they exclaimed.
"Dey is hard times ahead fer you an' fer we ; nobody ter feed us, nobody ter wait on missy! I
reckon we must all go home ter Green Forest;
we longs ter see de grey moss waving."

Until the hour arrived, we never suspected
what it would cost us to drive away from Pine
Knot, thus sundering ties and severing relation-

ships that, with happy memories, bound us to the past. We had been petted and spoiled by more than one black mammie.

To Ducpon, our new home, Belfast, Lawrence, and Georgia went with a wagon containing a few household effects. These they offered to put in order before our arrival. Dick was now at our gate with a rattling old carriage and two lazy mules. On the front cushion, where a nurse usually sat, were bundles and a home-made cage; inside a blue-bird hopping from perch to perch. Lunch, our house-pet, was securely tied in a bag. She scratched and meowed insistently.

"Good-bye, missy, God bless yer," said one negro after another. "Don't forgit we w'at's goin' home; send your old frocks an' massa's pants. Some one'll be glad fer dem." Juno's little girl Cissy, pulling at my gay balmoral, begged that she might have it.

All details settled, my husband proposed that we start. "Time and tide wait for no man!" said he. Then he asked for Lydia and the child?

"Sis Lyddy! "the women called," massa is ready ter git in de carriage. Sonnie, whey is you?"

Between sobs Juno said, "I reckon dey is in ma's cabin." She went herself in search of dem.

"Dey ain't deir," she cried. "Ma's box is

fling open, her clothes scattered on de floor. Oh !
whey is ma? She never leaves her box open;
hunno people, hunt ; dey's trouble somewhere,
caise las' night when Bro' Robin was sayin' he
wouldn't tol'rate any nonsense, ma make answer:
' Nobody shall drag me 'way from my boy. I'd
rather we died in each odder's arms.' "

Frenzied at the mere suggestion, I rushed into
the empty cabin, only to find glowing pine logs
hissing and singing. " Lydia, Lydia," I called,
" where are you with our child. Go quickly, one
of you, and tell Dick to drag the well. Oh ! they
must be there, or they would answer ! "

We found them behind the cabin built for the
loom. The little playhouse stood there with
its corn-cob soldiers, home-made toys, and clay
marbles. In close embrace the nurse was enfolding " her boy," his ruby lips pressed against her
dusky cheeks, his arms locked around her neck.
Of the excitement their absence was causing they
were both unconscious.

We started, finally, and after we were well along
our journey, I noticed in the pocket of my little
boy's kilt, an inlaid snuff-box, and recognised it
as one that had belonged to Lydia's master,
Squire Jameston. Snapping the cover to and
fro, delighted with his new toy, the child said,
" Mommer gave me this to keep for my glass

marbles she's going to send me from Tomshear. Oh, isn't mommer coming to put me to bed to-night? Mommer, please come! I won't go to sleep till you do," his little voice quivering with emotion.

A new life dawned upon us,—a veritable reality filled with bitter experiences and hardships. We faced stern facts with the energy of young minds, feeling that our future was what we had to deal with, not the past.

At the quaint little place Ducpon, Revilo held the office of Internal Revenue Collector. A stage-coach occasionally passed, dropping a mail bag, so bringing us in touch with the world again.

The post-office, we were told, was originally called Philanteska, an Indian name for the river near by, on the banks of which the red men once fished and hunted unmolested by whites. The story is, that the pioneer settlers, finding the name difficult to spell, as well as to pronounce, called a meeting to discuss a change of name. A full attendance was present, with Squire Weeks in the chair. Tossing his hat behind him he brought his fist down on the table. "Gentle-men," said he, "the object of comin' togedder is to make writin' easy. There is a blame lot of complaint in the settlement ober this blarsted name Pilantesca, brought here by red tomahawk

Injins. This court is open for suggestions from de benches. Don't be backward in speken your mind, only don't all riz to once."

A scrawney pineland cracker rose. "Is it a name you is a askin' for? Ever sense I moved to these diggins dis post-office has been a tarrification to my soul. Some words is hard to articulate, but this Pilantesca beats my time for spellen'. My boy Bill is at a highfaluten town school; he thinks he knows more than a judge, an' writes wid a steel pen. A gander's quill is good 'nough for the parson an' me. I 'lows when dis post-office slips from the pint of Bill's writin' stick, it's time for him to cum home an' help me fight rampacious grass in the corn-fields. This larned boy has writ for us to name the place Cypress Lake, after the wild duck pon' near by.

Down came the speaker's fist: " The word Cypress is afore the meeten."

Mounting a bench, a bow-legged dwarf lifted his hat, which he had neglected to remove. " Mr. Cheer, our larned brother brings forth a conjection. I is ransacking my brain to spell Cypress. Is it a dictionaire word ? "

Again the room reverberated from the force of another blow on the table. " The brother with the larned son will tell this here mceten the best way to spell Cypress," said the chairman.

Bill's father looked round, then rose slowly, yawning by way of gaining time. "That rascal," said he, "writ the word on a scrap of paper, but I'll be blowed if I kin find it." Each of his pockets he turned wrongside out, scattering rusty nails, twists of tobacco, a jack-knife, and broken links of an ox-chain. "Mr. Speaker," he cried, "you may hang me to a tree-limb if there ain't a y in the word, to middle or at the tail end, I swear I don't know."

The herb doctor of the settlement sat on the front seat, His shaggy overhanging brows, unshaven face, and wealth of sun-faded locks falling about his shoulders, added to the dignity of his massive figure. Running his hand through his hair, part of which remained on end, he drawled out, "If the chair will accept my conception of this intricate trouble, I'll move and second that we have a division. The lion's share of a name may be stuck on the post-office door. Then, sir, I names this new-born place Ducpon." He counted the six letters on his fingers. "No one will git sick spellen it."

Down came the chairman's fist. "Gentlemen, it's moved an' seconded. Those in favor, say Duc; those opposed, Cypress." With a look of intense satisfaction he counted the hands uplifted. "The Duc's has it," he yelled. "Now, we gentlemen of edication need not scratch our heads, spill the ink, an' turn goose quills backward a spellen this here post-office ; thanks to Dr. Will Pitts Premier."

Thus it was that our letters were post-marked " Ducpon."

Poverty, with one decisive stride, had entered our dwelling. Pride, accordingly, should have flown out the window, as love is wont to do. But Love wound its arms a wee bit tighter, and pride hid its head, going bravely yet blindly to work.

Our front steps and piazza in the days of slavery were swept before breakfast. Johanna, our woman of all work at Ducpon, having a hot meal to prepare before eight, had no time for early cleaning. Unaccustomed to such work I, on the other hand, was not strong enough to wield a broom until fortified with food.

While I swept after breakfast, Revilo's father, who lived across the way, comforted himself with a corncob pipe and the Virginia weed, his heels on the piazza rail, in genuine Southern style. Swallow Cote, his home, had been bought with Confederate money, but was now for sale,—cheap for green-backs.

The second week of February the post brought me from New York a flaming comic valentine, representing Bridget in gay dress, arms akimbo, her broom resting against the steps. We were all greatly amused, and wondered how my recently industrious moods could be known in New York. Like Brer Rabbit, however, I "lay low," awaiting my turn for a practical joke.

A northern man was visiting Colonel Ross in the neighbourhood, for the express purpose of investing in southern lands. Almost every estate below Mason and Dixon's line at that date was for sale; so the arrival of a man with surplus capital caused considerable talk in our community. No one, however, knew the newcomer's name. A few spoke of him as Colonel Humphries, others as Major Humbert, of Bull Run fame.

March winds expended their fury, and Judge Floyd convened the spring term of Court at Old Town, as in days before the war. Colonel Bee— Revilo's father, once a prominent lawyer of Savernake—was retained by Widow Lamb to defend her case. There was still a chill in the night air, endangering young cotton and corn, making lawyer's fees, accordingly, more doubtful. Notwithstanding discouragements, the judge and his advocates were in a gay mood, sitting around a pine-knot fire in the village-tavern, smoking their corncob pipes. A belated stage-coach rattled up to the door.

In the centre of the table was one tallow candle, which gave but a feeble light. The men, how-. ever, amused each other by telling stories of thrilling adventures or of funny incidents in their recent camp-life.

A shout of merriment had followed a yarn told by Captain Wynn, when the portly pro-prietor entered with a handful of letters : " Six for Judge Floyd, four for Colonel Bee, Captain Wynn, Lieutenant Terrell," and so on, calling off the names of many ex-Confederate officers. (Smooth-flowing ink and Irish linen had induced wives and sweethearts to write long letters.)

No word was spoken for a time. Young lawyer Terrell was slyly pressing his fiancée's tinted pages to his lips, when Colonel Bee suddenly sprang to his feet, exultingly waving a gilt-edged blue sheet.

" Gentlemen, I hope you have each as good news as I. Before the war, I opened business letters first, Now it's reversed ; home-news must be read to brace one up for disappointments that follow each other like cannon balls."

Fixing his keen black eyes on young Terrell, he said :

" That billet-doux was sweet, was it ? Well, wait forty years ; then the woman who has stood beside you in cloud or sunshine will pen words more tender than any written by the fairest maiden in her teens. After reading my dear wife's news, this last—real business letter!—has made my head reel, and I'm beside myself with anticipated happiness. Your pockets, like mine, are empty, I reckon, and the thermometer of hope stands somewhere about zero, but, with money in hand, pleasures will quickly return.

"Your Honour, won't you call to order, that I may read aloud my letter?" He waved the tinted pages overhead.

Judge Floyd gave the order.

There was a suspicion of tear-drops on the colonel's glasses ; then he read aloud :

The Wigwam, Mch. 31st, 1866.

Colonel Bee :

Dear Sir,—Through a friend I learn that Swallow Cote is for sale. Kindly let me know your lowest cash price. I am prepared to make you an offer of one thousand dollars, with two notes additional of five hundred each, payable yearly.

As I'm leaving for New York, grant me an early response.

Yours respectfully,

JAMES HUMBERT (Major.)

Out of their seats the lawyers bounded, scream-

16

ing "Hurrah! Three cheers for Colonel Bee
and his good luck!"

Hearing an unusual stir, the proprietor pushed
open the door.

" Hello!" the men cried, " hello! cigar-vender,
bring us a box of your best Havanas, and charge
them to Colonel Bee's account."

Corncob pipes were tossed on the floor: one
who had the prospect of selling southern land
could supply cigars. Since the guns of Fort
Sumter belched their grape-shot, these were the
first many had smoked.

" Colonel, how we would like to be in your
shoes, with a thousand dollars of Uncle Sam's
green paper to spend."

More than one begged, " Turn over your law
cases to me."

Lawyer Wren patted his moneyless purse.
With a sigh he declared that, "hope deferred"
had made his " heart sick." " Colonel Bee," he
continued, "a few of your cases would quite
revive me."

Men of dignity, like school children, divided the
contents of the cigar-box, sniffing the compressed
weed with an unutterable sensation of satisfaction. Lawyers and Methodist parsons have a
wonderful faculty for enjoying their circuit work.

While the empty cigar-box blazed in the fire,

these defenders of the law bade each other good-night.

Colonel Bee, to pay for his treat, roused the nodding clerk, and placed before him a ten-dollar bill,—Widow Lamb's retaining fee.

The next day was Sunday, a fair and sunny April day. Parson Hill's text—"Whatsoever ye shall ask in my name, that will I do"—seemed almost prophetic. And the hymn

> " Prayer is the soul's sincere desire,
>   Uttered or unexpressed ;
> The motion of a hidden fire
>   That trembles in the breast,"

at least by one, was sung with deep feeling. Indeed, many looked round to see whose voice was so rich and full. Later Colonel Bee, himself the singer, once or twice took out his papers that day to be sure the letter was there. Early training restrained him, however, from reading a business communication on the Sabbath.

Young Terrell Sunday afternoon covered pages with loving words to his future bride. Colonel Bee wrote to his wife :

Old Town Tavern,
April 1st, 1866.

Darling Wife :—
Like an angel of peace for forty years you have

ministered to me. God bless you! In the clash of arms, with bullets whizzing about the heads of our boys, no murmur escaped your lips. The Lord be praised for such a wife and mother! In our poverty, brought about by that crazy philanthropist, Abe. Lincoln, you have greeted me day after day with a smile. Now, I hope the sun is about to shine on our silvering locks. I haven't many on the top of my head, but you have. I had a letter last night from Maj. Humbert,—by the way, do you remember I told you he was not called Col. Humphries,—offering to buy Swallow Cote, paying one thousand cash with two notes of five hundred dollars each. We will now be able to return to Savernake and begin the old life again.

I will follow this letter on Tuesday. Judge Floyd has agreed to place Widow Lamb's case first on the docket to-morrow, so I may finish my defense before returning to draw and sign the papers for that rich Yankee. I do believe I can bring myself to say ' God bless him ! ' the fellow.

Yours till death,

Harvey.

P. S.—Say to my industrious daughter-in-law across the way, that I will present her with a new improved ladies' broom, and a copper dust-pan.

Happiness fires young life into excitement,

often dispelling sleep.   Older minds, on the contrary, are soothed into refreshing slumber.   The
colonel not coming down to breakfast at the
usual hour on Monday morning, the waiter—expecting a generous fee—tapped at his door : " I's
hot coffee an' bacon an' eggs waiting fer you, sah."

The judge and eleven of the jurors were in
their places in court at nine o'clock.

Colonel Bee, hastily arranging his papers, caught
sight of Major Humbert's letter.

" Before the twelfth man comes," he thought,
" I'll be able to answer this for the noon post."
He writes :

In Court.

Maj. Humbert,
    Dear Sir :—
        *I thank you for your kind letter containing
an offer for Swallow Cote, which I accept. If
nothing prevents I will return on Tuesday, prepared
to make you a deed of sale,*

Yours respectfully,
Harvey C. Bee (Colonel).

To be sure that the title was Major and not
Colonel, he withdrew the letter from its envelope,
and ran his eye over its pages.

Streaming in through blindless windows, the

clear sunlight revealed the small word "over," in the left-hand corner.

Judge Floyd sounded three loud raps and announced, "This court is convened!" after which Parson Hill lifted his voice in prayer.

Colonel Bee reverently leaned forward, his elbows on the desk, his forehead clasped by his interlocked palms.

The prayer concluded, the clerk arose: "Your Honour, by your order the case of Bullock versus Lamb is placed first on the docket."

The summing-up of this noted case had been looked forward to with keen interest. Savernake's gifted lawyer, with a new joy in his heart, would now doubtless surpass his former brilliancy of speech.

In her fresh spring-mourning, widow Lamb sat in the dock, her cheeks rosy red.

Down came the judge's gavel.

"The summing-up of the defence will now be heard," he said.

The widow's advocate appeared to be intently reading an open letter. He moved not a muscle.

Tapping the colonel on the shoulder, lawyer Wren leaned forward and whispered, "Your case is called."

Colonel Bee rose slowly, with a dazed look, altogether unlike his usually animated manner. Without regarding the judge, he addressed the twelve men seated to the right of Judge Floyd : " Gentlemen, I thank you for your close attention, but the summing-up now is of no consequence, for my daughter-in-law has won. She has paid me one thousand dollars, with two notes and interest." Lifting his hand to his forehead, as if to collect his thoughts, he bowed to the judge and dropped into his chair, murmuring, " It's a Valentine versus April Fool."

The lawyers, fearing sudden illness, rushed to his side. Terrell, with keen eye, caught sight of the words, " You are an April Fool," written on the inside of a blue gilt-edge sheet of letter paper.

Recalling that the day for playing tricks had but just past, he instantly interpreted the joke,— the proposed sale of Swallow Cote.

He handed the letter to the judge.

XIX.

Sara once a Good Wife.

"She doeth little kindnesses,
Which most leave undone or despise."
LOWELL.

DURING the years of our refuge in the piney
woods, our pigs often brought forth more
young than they could rear, hence the
little velvety creatures were ruthlessly destroyed,
to the horror of poor Juno. Impoverished as we
were, there was always some waste, so we agreed
between us that she should feed them on the
kitchen refuse, and divide the number of pigs
fattened.

When freedom dawned, Juno had five fat pigs
almost ready for slaughter. Lydia and her family
would at least have meat for a time.

Robin smacked his lips in anticipation of blood
pudding, spare ribs, and sausages.

Matthew, our man of all work, one afternoon
presented his brother, a " Mr. White " who was
buying pigs. " Mr. White " held in his hand a
great roll of greenbacks.

Eve was tempted beyond her powers of resistance, and so was I. Our home at Ducpon was barren of every comfort, and the mere sight of money tempted me to sell, so when " Mr. White " made a formal offer of fifty dollars for my pigs, I accepted it. Tea cups, chairs, and warm underwear were now within reach.

Revilo had made no end of fun of the copartnership between Juno and me. Now he realised that unless he could produce a like amount of negotiable money for the privilege of shedding swine's blood, the bacon would hang in another's smoke-house.

The bargain with " Mr. White "—whose face was as black as a coal—was hardly made when my husband tilted his creaking old rocking-chair forward, whispering, " Your pigs were worth at least seventy-five dollars."

" Why, then, did you let me take fifty if I could have gotten more."

" You never consulted me in your anxiety to finger those dirty bills. I have learned by experience never to give a woman advice unless she requests it."

Matthew and his guest had a hearty supper in our kitchen, and " Mr. White's " horse a good feed in the stable. Matthew tapped at the door about bed-time. " Please, sah, kin Mr. White spend de night wid me. De pigs ain't come up yit; dey ranges a good way eaten pine-mas.' "

"All right, Matthew," I called. "The receipt will be written and signed when you bring the money."

At the prospect of comforts in the house our hopes revived, even as grass springs into fresh life after a spell of drought.

We listened, at early dawn, for the squeal of pigs, which—unlike lambs led to the slaughter—sound their own death-knell.

The receipt I had signed lay on our table, but no one came for it: Matthew had gone early in search of the pigs.

"Mr. White," after a hasty breakfast, left word with Johanna that he would return in two days. Matthew reached home at noon, on his face a weary look; his search had been fruitless. He seemed sure, however, that the pigs were taken up by some one for a reward, as had been the case with our pet pony Ella.

"Mr. White" returned to Pine Knot twice the following week, but each time taking away with him his soiled greenbacks.

Two weeks after his last visit I was called to the door one night. Sam, a former slave at Swallow Cote, desired to speak with me.

As solemnly as if kissing a Bible, he said:

" Missy, it take niggers fer ter ketch up wid niggers. Hearin' 'bout de loss o' your bacon hogs, I's spotted a fellow singin' hallelujah in Zion's gate. He has most on de time a greasy mouth; we honest folks is bleeged now ter eat dry hoecake, caise we has no massa ter feed us. In conjitation I has come to de conclus dat I kin put my finger-tips on your salted meat."

Thinking of my teacups, I assured Sam he would be well rewarded if he found my pigs, dead or alive.

" It's not fer money I does it, ma'am ; it's fer ole time sake."

" Let it be as you wish, only find them."

Sam scratched his head, jerked up his suspenders, and showed plainly that there was something more he wished to confide.

" Missy, as I has de 'tention ter bring you comf'ting news, can't you loan me a dollar? Den I kin gib de hunt 'tire justice. It's a delicate matter, an' I mus' handle it like a new-born baby, an' so can't go ter my work ter-morrow, when I mus' split rails ter git some cash, caise if dere's a pound o' meat in de cabin I don't know it, nor a quart ob meal in de cupboard. By de next day your pigs may be carted off ter Old Town. I dassent go home empty-handed an' pull de latch-string. Sara used ter be a good wife in Slavery

time.   Now de fus word is, 'What's you got ter
eat?'   Colonel Ross is off'ring fifty cents a day
fer wemen.   When I 'ludes ter it, Sara glares at
me an' says: 'Is you forgot Mars Abe Linkum
set we free? We is ter be ladies like de w'ite foks.
Does you want your wife ter work like a slave
nigger? Massa's gals don't hoe in de co'nfields.
I's free as dey is, an' don't 'ten' ter chop cotton or
co'n fer no w'ite man. I's a free lady. I'll cook an'
help eat what you brings, will wash your clo's
if dey ain't too bloody wid butcherin', an' if you
comes wid a chicken or watermillion I'll put a
patch in your breeches. Write down in your book,
Sam, Sara's a slave no longer. I's waitin' now
ter eat wid gold spoons, dat I is.'   I has a wife
like dat now, ma'am."

Sam left my door with a dollar on account.

Days and weeks passed, as they usually pass in
rural districts.   Our plant of hope had withered.
Once more, however, Sam asked for a confidence.
"I find dese bristles in de woods," he whispered,
handing me a small paper package; "de groun'
is red wid blood. Keep quiet, ma'am, I has my
eyes on a shoutin' chu'ch sinner; he's out o'
work, but his mouth is greasy all de same. I
dassent tell his name yit, caise free niggers don't
take no 'count of a man's life, poppin' a fellow
back of he head plum' ter kingdom come."

In the piney woods, all around the altar of sacrifice, valuable blood had been shed, yet no gleam of light revealed the fact to me.

The kitchen garden was forced into life by a southern sun ; and spring advanced. Matthew should be planting peas and beans. I called him.

Johanna said she had not seen him. In fact, he was in his cabin, tossing with a high fever. Accordingly, we summoned a doctor and a coloured nurse, ourselves each day ministering to his needs.

One afternoon, finding him partly conscious, I repeated in his hearing a few Scripture texts.

Great black hands reached out and a pitiful wail escaped his parched lips: "I can't die! Do, Miss Bee, forgive me?"

"Be calm, Matthew," said I. "Ask God's forgiveness, not mine."

But he insisted. "Say you forgive me, ma'am. Oh, I can't die till I tell you! Uncle Sam an' me kill your pigs an' Mr. White carted de meat to Hatville. Oh, forgive me!"

His penitence touched me, as I was sure that his end was approaching. He received my full and free pardon. Exhausted, he then swooned into unconsciousness.

Much to the doctor's astonishment, the next

day he found Matthew had passed the crisis—he would live. No reference was made to his confession; we waited for his recovery.

He was missed from his cabin one morning. Wheel-tracks showed that he had been taken away by night, with his possessions. We had physician and nurse to pay. His wages, too, he had drawn in full before his illness,—" Mr. White's " roll of money possibly.

Sam swore to his innocence : " Dat fool fellow dyin' got my name suffused wid some no 'count rascal. Don't 'sociate your fam'ly niggers wid such shameful 'ceedings."

I believed him.

Swallow Cote was finally sold. Colonel Bee, the silvery-haired lawyer, who effected the sale, sent to me, as a mark of sympathy, a gift of plates, platters, cups, and saucers of one hue; also a rocking-chair and dust-pan.

XX.

Lydia and Marlborough Meet.

"Dig the grave and let me lie
Glad did I live and gladly die."
—R. L. Stevenson.

THE first news we received of Lydia, came in a letter written by a lady in Tomshear. She tried to write it as nearly as possible according to Lydia's dictation.

Tomshear, Ga., Jan., 1866.

My dear Missy,

An' my Sonnie,

When you drove off I went straight in de cabin an' turned de button. I didn't want ter see nobody. I sat on de bare floor huggin' my corncob soldier Sonnie told me ter keep, kissin' dose clay marbles shinin' wid his finger-marks. Outside Juno was breakin' her heart cryin' " Ma, Bro' Robin is come, an' your t'ings is fling out on de flo'." I make answer : ' My byadier silk is all I cares fer." Bro' Robin hit his fist on de dooc. " I's hongry," says he, " I wants my dinner." I open de dooe, cooked de hoecake an' tried ter eat; but it lodged 'long side my palate. De mens built a rail fence round de three graves, den we all started fer Tomshear, wid my mule an' wagon massa give me. I couldn't walk far, so had ter ride wid de chilluns, fryin' pans an' boxes. It want easy goin' like when " my boy " was settin' in my lap in de carriage. Campin' out has give me rhumatis in my legs. I'm crippled a good part of de time. I trembles fer ter-morrow an' next day caise Bro' Robin ain't patient like Bro' Molbro. If dey had only left me under de pines! I knows how Miss Dodo will trouble when she hears mommer ain't well. I am trying not ter fret. Bro' Robin an' Dick has hired a tumblerdown shanty. I ain't used ter live in a house wid so many; not ter tell 'bout de dirty clo's folks give us ter wash an' iron. Dick's pa is gitting worse, but Juno can't travel. Mars Dr. Sam is here, an' promises ter 'tend her. He says it makes him t'ink o' Green Forest ter see us. Juno frets lots; she says she knows she's going ter die.

Sonnie, write me a letter, an' put a kiss so mommer kin press her lips on de spot where her baby's mouth was. Have you got pants on yit? Send them ter me ter wash. I'll flute de ruffles missy said she was 'tending ter put up de outside **seams.**

De folks all sends heap a howdy.

I's longin' fer your picture, Sonnie. Tell massa de blin' mule pulled like a man on de long heavy roads cut up by Yankees' big wagons. We came near upsettin' lots o' times. I's hoping ter go ter Green Forest, so I keeps de mule tied behin' de shanty. It stamps so hard sometimes I can't sleep. We dassent turn it loose ter graze, so many free niggers is roamin' round. Bro' Molbro has jes lost his youngest boy. I's longin' ter console him ; he's livin' at Lamont's, his mother 'tending ter de chilluns. This letter is writ from the heart of

Your loving mommer,

Lyddy."

Our fears were confirmed, Robin's family were now in a great measure dependent upon money earned by our nurse. Having climbed her mountain of life, with no hard work to do, this constant drudgery at the wash-tub hastened her down the plane. We were powerless, save to spare what money we could from my husband's meagre salary.

Month after month accounts grew more depressing. When Dick and Juno's infant, Josephine, was old enough to travel, they set out for Siberty County.

Jim lived but a short time after their arrival.

17

Georgia now married Abel. James was working on the railroad.

When General Grant issued his Ironclad Oath, Revilo returned his unsigned, and of course lost his position as a government official. This pre-vented us from assisting Lydia with money.

Removing to northern Georgia, we wrote for her to come to us, hoping that the bracing air would invigorate her. We offered to share with her our last crumb.

Her reply showed the true devotion that per-meated her soul.

August, 1866.

My dear Massa :—

I would 'cept of your kind invitation ter come an' live wid you, but mommer can't even sweep de steps. My feet is swollen twice deir size; it's all I kin do ter stand long 'nough ter iron de shirt-fronts fer Georgia. She is doin' de plain ironin' well.

De weather is hotter dan I eber 'members ter feel it. If missy could give me one dose of medicine wid her own hands, perhaps I'd git better. Bro' Mol-bro sent word if we didn't start at once he'd come heself ter bring me ter Green Forest, where Sis Nannie an' Tim Cay is livin'. How is your eyes, massa ? I knows you has a hard time, an' soon " my sonny " mus' be goin' ter college, like odder young gen'men. I was so glad fer de picture you sent me.

He is a sure 'nough man now, in pantaloons, wid his curls cut.

T'ank you, massa, fer de money. I kisses eb'ry bill, caise I knows you needs it. I keeps " my boy's" picture under my pillow, an' Bro' Robin says if I kiss it much more dere won't be any marks left.

> *Your faithful servant,*
>
> *Lyddy.*

Months doubled and tripled; in fact, it was a year before Lydia started for the goal of her desire. From her bed came often the simple strains of an old plantation song, " 'Way down upon de Swanee riber."

Their tedious journey to Green Forest was nearing its end, when the mule suddenly stopped, refusing to go one step farther in the dark. The party halted beside the road, and, lighting a camp-fire, settled for the night.

Lydia's cup of delight seemed brimming over, when, at dawn, she aroused the sleeping caravan, "We is at Navarre, dere is de big gate, all tumble down! de avenue plum' full o' weeds. Oh! I mus' go an' see de house if it is in ruin."

Lawrence and Lucy assisted her.

At sight of the ungainly chimneys, in the midst of a pile of ashes,—all that remained of a home where, thirty years before, she had awaited her master's young bride,—she burst into tears.

"Gib me a handful o' dat sacred ashes, Lawrence, an' promise me you'll strew it in my open grave."

"Oh, ma, you mus'n't die!" he cried. "Do send for missy, she kin make you well; you mus'n't die."

"It's too late, my son," she responded. "It's too late. If I could have stayed wid dem I might have lived dese many a year. Nobody is ter blame but me. Don't forgit, Lawrence, if you plants corn when de shocks is brown, you'll have corn, but, if you sows tares, dey won't be a grain o' wheat. I had a good master an' missus; deir coachman ready ter wait on me day an' night; yet my head got turned by a yaller free-nigger, he promisin' silks an' satins, wid my own house an' maid. I hates free niggers. 'Pears ter me massa is free, not we, caise we must work harder dan eber. Where is my freedom? I was nebei sech a slave. My feet is tied tighter dan Peter's when de angel struck de fetters an' said, 'Go free, Peter!' It won't be long afore an angel will break my bands."

"Ma, what's you talkin' 'bout? Do come an' lie down in de wagon; hear Bro' Robin's a-yellin' fer us now."

On the way to Green Forest, the lazy mule jogging along, Lydia sang another old song, changed to suit herself:

> "We are almost there, we are almost there,
> Said a dying slave as she neared home;
> Where are the trees that grew just here,
> Where is the moss hanging on each cone?"

Nannie, hearing that they were near Green Forest, arranged a pallet beside her blazing hearth. Tim Cay chopped the weeds around the next cabin, to be occupied by Robin and his family.

Scarcely waiting to greet any of her former associates on her arrival, Lydia cried, "Dis is not my massa's Green Forest. Whey is we house wid de yaller brick steps? Whey is Uncle Frank's chu'ch? Whey is de gin-house where ' my chilluns' played in de loose cotton? Is my eyes blin', Sis' Nannie? Dis is not we Green Grove. I don't smell magnolias, jassemine an' orange blossoms. Is not one left ter show where my cabin stood wid de bell-rope stretchin' 'cross ter de nuss'ry? Bro' Molbro an' me'll never sit under we own vine an' fig-tree ag'in!"

The day wore on. Robin and Tim were busy patching the roof of Machiah's house, when a tall, slender black man, his head tinged with grey, quietly entered Nannie's cabin. No one was in but a woman asleep on a pallet,—a mere shadow of her former self. He knelt, winding his arms about her. Startled, she returned the embrace : "De Lord's name be praised! If here ain't Bro' Molbro!"

At that inopportune moment Robin flung open the door, not knowing of his brother's arrival.

"Is dat de way you kin use your arms? I t'ought you was crippled wid rhumatis, an' dis long time ain't washed a pocket-henkerchief fer a fellow. 'Pears to me you's clutchin' dat shirt-collar purty tight."

"Oh, Bro' Robin," and her arms dropped on her breast, "can't you 'low me one minute's joy wid we coachman? We growed up togedder ; we loved massa an he bride. Bro' Molbro's voice brings my w'ite chilluns runnin' into my arms, de two gals cryin' in de rice-field trunk, Tom an' Jerry switchin' deir tails an' stampin' by de saw-mill. Dose days we was sittin' under we own vine an' fig-tree. Now we's both suff'rin'. But it won't be long ; spare me one leedle hour ob joy, Bro' Robin."

"Have all you want ; I has no 'jection, you's no 'count in de cabin. You might go to Lamont's, caise Flora ain't dere ter talk 'bout your black pair of wings."

Springing to his feet, Marlborough shook his

fist in his brother's face: "I wish I'd smashed your skull fer you years ago," he cried. "Ter t'ink you dares call my Lyddy your wife! Git out o' dis room or I'll poun' your head into jelly."

"Put de weight o' your toe-nail on me an' you'll fin' your match. Your hair is grey, an' I's a free nigger."

The underpinning giving way, Tim Cay called for assistance,—leaving the lovers alone.

"Lyddy, my darlen, com' wid me to Lamont's; be my wife; I'll take care of you," said Marlborough; "gib you a comf'table home an' my gal Flora will wait on you like a maid. I has no carriage nor silk frocks ter offer, but when you can't walk I'll take you in my strong arms. Lyddy, I has loved you all my life. If marriages is made in heaven, like massa used to read, why is dis ring"—breaking the threads holding it in his waistcoat front—"been waitin' fer ober twenty years ter go on your finger? It has 'Lyddy' writ inside, so soap an' water won't wash it out.' —He patted her crippled hand.—"Let me put it on now, then we'll be j'ined. You will be my wife."

"Flora is buried," she replied, "but Bro' Robin is livin', an' Mars C. C. said 'so long as you both lives. Massa neber broke no marriages. He's dead an' gone, but his voice rings in my ear.

Las' night while we was sleepin' by Navarre, an'
we didn't know it, I dreamed I heard him call me,
saying, 'Lyddy, here's your young missy. I's
going ter look ter you dat she neber wants fer
anyt'ing.' Den in my sleep I hugged her tiny
feet an' kissed dem. An' her soft w'ite hand patted me on my bandanna; her sweet voice said,
'I'm goin' ter be good ter you as long as I live.'
God knows she was! I ain't 'shamed, Bro' Molbro, ter tell you I has always loved you eber since
we used ter sit side by side in de kitchen at Navarre. 'Cordin' ter de angel-voice hissin' in de
chimney-jamb, I has tied myself; but it won't be
long. I often hears rumblin' charyot wheels, so
I is sure de winged horses is on de way. When
my strength gits low, take my finger an' put on
de ring wid de gol' mark. My wings has been
stained wid sin, but de Lord kin wash dem w'ite.
I has not been your wife in de Green Forest, but
in Paradise Christ will gib us a mansion not made
wid hands; roamin' dere we'll meet we w'ite folks
we loved so well."

She smiled, as a thought came to mind. "Was
dat de dagger I was afraid of?" pointing to the
ring. "There'll be no fightin' dere; no tears, no
separations."

Clasping her wasted form to his heart Marlborough kissed her. "Lyddy, my heart's wife,

wid pure w'ite wings, I'll keep de ring here,"— tapping his waistcoat—"till de sweet charyot swings low. Dat word massa gave us, 'God is love', is neber out o' my min'. When we meets in Paradise we'll tell him we has found it 's true."

XXI.

A Marriage in Heaven.

"A soul as white as heaven."
BEAUMONT AND FLETCHER.

THE Utopian days of Green Forest were past ; its principal buildings in ashes. The sawmill, too, was fallen into decay, the door of the " Jewish Synagogue" lay on the ground, its hinges rusty and weather-beaten. Here and there a Cherokee rose showed where a hedge surrounded the well and the moss-covered bucket, now constantly on the dip, quenching the thirst of freemen. One narrow trodden path, in the midst of rank weeds, marked where bare little black feet trotted back and forth with wooden pails and piggins.

Enriched with soldier and negro bones a line of cedars, well matured, blended rich green with silvery grey moss.

Lydia was not strong enough to roam in the grove. Marlborough wheeled her once in a barrow to where tall chimneys stood, sentinel-like

over the past.   On a charred rafter they sat chat-
ting of bygone happiness, when food and raiment
were had for the mere acceptance.   In weakness,
her head rested upon her lover's shoulder.   Overhead, as gayly as ever, mocking birds sang as they
had sung twenty years before.   With his soul's
wife in his arms, Marlborough was happier than
he had been for years.   Yet he felt sure Lydia
could not last many weeks.

"I was de happiest man in Siberty County before Marmaduke came to plaster dese walls," he
said.

Toying in the débris, he unearthed an iron nut-
cracker.   Fire had melted its silver coating.

" Bro'   Marlbro," Lydia asked,   "does you,
'member de night massa came from Savernake
wid a box o' silver?   Dis was in it; he neber
forgot us; you had a silber-handle carriage-whip,
an' I a new cradle fer ' my baby ' " ;—she thought
for a moment ;—"it was my Letha, wid de black
ringlets on her pretty head.   Has all dat silber
turned to ashes ?"

" Neber min', my Lyddy, in de mansions not
made wid han's we won't want gold or silber.
Mars C. C. said de streets was paved wid crystals
sparklin' like di'monds, an' God sittin' on a great
w'ite t'rone."

Drawing from her bosom a well-thumbed

carte-de-visite photograph, Lydia covered it with kisses.

"You neber saw my little man in frilled pantaloons, after he could talk an' tell his mommer how much he loved her.   I tried not ter let Miss Dodo know how my heart was breakin' caise Bro' Robin wouldn't let me stay.   I opened de cabin dooe eb'ry mornin' wid a laugh on my face; but inside was tears ready ter fall like rain.   Juno has promised ter put my byadier silk on me, an' you my ring wid de gol' mark, den lay dis pictur' an' my corncob soldier jes where Sonnie's golden curls used ter lie.   De clay marbles"—counting one by one from her pocket—" put dem in de folds of my bur'yal robe.   Wheel me home, Bro' Molbro, I must lay me down ter sleep, I'm so tired."

Not many days after, Juno, with Boy leaning on her knee, rubbed her mother's cold hands. But no friction could warm them.   Stroking her chill brow, Marlborough sat silent, great tear-drops running down his black cheeks.   Nannie stirred a pot of gruel, hoping to revive her sister-in-law. Dazed by a strange scene of approaching dissolution, Edward stood at the foot of the bed; while outside, Lawrence hurriedly cut wood to warm the room.

" Is dis you, Juno ? " Lydia said in a faint voice.

" Hold ma's hand. Molbro,"—and she tried to look into his face,—" I hears de rumblin' o' charyot wheels,—de sweet charyot. Sissy, Boy," —then for a moment all was still—" my pic-tur'. My sold-ier—my marbles."

Encircling her form with his left arm, his lips near hers, Marlborough removed Lucy's ring from her finger and tossed it into the fire. In its place he put one marred by contact with intense heat. " Lyddy, my wife, my angel, wid snow-w'ite wings tipped wid silber," he whispered, " you are mine, forever mine, fer God is love ! "

Nannie asked, " Shall I call Bro' Robin ? "

With one word Marlborough forbade her.

Braced by that unaccountable energy that frequently proceeds dissolution, Lydia lifted her left hand and kissed the ring. In a voice scarcely audible, she spoke : " As de eyes of servants look ter de hand of deir master, an' de eyes of a maid ter de hand of her mistress, so, Lord, my eyes is waitin' on dee. Molbro, my husband, in heaven we'll meet ! " A smile showed her double row of pearly teeth. Her inanimate body rested in her lover's warm embrace.

Juno and Lawrence insisted that " if missy had given Ma medicine wid her own han's, she wouldn't 'a' died."

Lydia lay stretched upon a deal bench, her

hands enfolding a white boy's picture, a sheet thrown lightly over her body. Her stiffened form was placed in a rude coffin made by Marlborough, Tim Cay, and Dick. With an eye to the future, Robin touched the gold band on her hand. "Shall I take off my ring ? "

" Dat ring shall be buried wid her. She wished it." Marlborough's stern voice silenced his brother.

One clay marble rolled to the dead one's feet from the pocket of the byadier silk.

Four men carried the coffin to the cedar enclosure. Marlborough, with Juno on his arm, walked as chief mourner, Nannie and Robin following.

Frank prayed earnestly. Then he announced his text "from de songs of David: ' Aldo we has been among de pots, yet shall we wings be like a dove's, kivered wid silber, de fedders like fine gol'. From hence she shall eat angels' food, fer God is love. De charyots also o' God is thousands of angels, an He has sent forth he winged host fer dis dear sister; she loved we master's family an' his people."

The body was lowered into the grave. Marlborough sprinkled a handful of dust over the coffin, saying, " Dis is de ashes of Navarre, where we nurse was once so happy. Now she's wid her master an' his bride. Friends, she was my wife

by rights. When de swect charyot swings low
fer me, I hopes ter lie here 'longside de purest
woman dat eber lived. I has waited fer twenty
years. Now she's got my ring on wid a name
writ inside wid a pen of fire. In heaven Lyddy
is my wife. God is love; blessed is His name.
Amen ! "

"Amen ! Amen !" responded the crowd, and
sobs heaved from many breasts.

Marlborough's undying love was in strange con-
trast to Robin's conduct. In a few weeks the
man, whom a seeming supernatural influence
had forced Lydia to marry, took to his cabin
another wife, Hetty, widow of Jim.

Marlborough's face had been overcast for years.
Now a deeper gloom settled there. Only once
did it become radiant ; and that was when, at
Lamont's, his daughter Flora and Lawrence were
pronounced man and wife.

" My chilluns," said he, "de Lord gib you de
joy Lyddy an' me should've had."

The blossoms that perfumed the air at Green
Forest are all dead. Not one green offshoot
of the myrtle remains. Lydia's master and
" baby boy " survived her but a few years. And
while " no marble marks her couch of lowly sleep,"
yet in the hearts of her " w'ite chilluns," down to
their grandchildren, her name is forever enshrined.

XXII.

Green Forest Sold at Auction.

"Calm 'mid the bewild'ring cry,
Confident of victory."

THE taxes on Green Forest land, year by
year, doubled and increased. Letha and
I, joint-owners in our widowhood, were
unable to cancel these formidable amounts.
Hence, a Federal tax-collector one morning galloped through the tangled moss-grown avenue
and nailed in conspicuous places three printed
bills.

John, a more capable rail-splitter than scholar,
tried to decipher the words, perspiring freely over
the effort. "By Jingo," he cried, "dem blue-
coats is offerin' we plantation fer sale! Dey
'tend ter turn de las' one o' us out dese cabins!"

Crowds gathered about him, gazing with untutored eyes upon the hieroglyphics. No one
thought of buying; it was beyond their ken.
Tim Cay, however, consulted with Marlborough
as to their best course if evicted.

One clear June day, three months after rain had spluttered on, and sunshine faded, the lettering of this—to us—cruel order, three horsemen arrived, and stuck upon the well-pole a bright red flag.

The Confederate and the Yankee flag the negroes were familiar with, but this blood-red rag—"What is it?" said they—"de devil's henkerchief?"

Marlborough was there, holding in his arms his granddaughter, Lyddy, who brought to his sad face the light of a new love.

One of the officers borrowed a wooden bench, mounted it, and cried aloud, as if to a crowd of eager purchasers, "Fifty acres of land is for sale! Who bids?"

Not a sound, save a cough or a sigh. Marlborough stood, hat in hand, in courtesy to what was happening on his master's old plantation.

"Does no one bid for this valuable land," continued the auctioneer? You black men, make me an offer; if it is only a fat pig. I must have a start."

Frank, accustomed to lead, stepped forward: "Boss,"—and he lifted his hat,—"I hopes you'll excuse me, but has you forgot dis place was bought from ole man Hamm by we massa? It's de finest estate in Siberty County, an' it hurts we niggers' feelin's fer you ter ask us fer a fat pig when de

18

goodest man dat eber lived paid down a pile of gol' dollars fer it."

"You old fool, if you've no money, keep your confounded talk to yourself. We are here to do our duty. Money is what we've come for, and we intend to get it. Does no one bid?"—noticing that Marlborough and Tim Cay whispered together—"You men over there, give me a bid!"

Marlborough put his little girl down before addressing a white man, and timidly replied, " Boss, Tim Cay an' me'll gib all we has, if you'll wait on us fer de balance."

"How much have you? Don't be afraid to speak! We are here to help you, not harm you. You look to be a sensible man; bid for this valuable land. Who bids?"

Tim Cay looked at his brother-in-law, scratched his head, and shot a squirt of tobacco juice to one side. "I reckon it will count nigh on ter twenty-five dollars, when I sells my pig an' Molbro his pony," said he.

"Twenty-five dollars is bid for fifty acres of Green Forest land! Does no one bid higher? Going, going, gone,—fifty acres is knocked down to—what's your name, sir?"

"Molbro."

"Mr. Molbro! Is that who I must make the deeds for?"

"I's plain Molbro Janes, I neber had a mister ter my name all dese years. I don't want one now."

"Slade, draw up the deed for Molbro Janes, coloured. I thought he was a sensible fellow. I find he's as big a fool as the biggest."

Scuse me, boss, will you bleege me by stakin' my part over yonder, where does cedar trees is; de balance, wid one cabin, you kin stick Tim Cay's title on."

"The deuce! What do you want with that enclosure? It looks confoundedly like a grave-yard! The ground is rich with dead bones; do you hope to grow corn ten feet high, with four ears to each stalk! Is that your idea?"

"I has no 'tention of growing' corn, boss. I did plant a sweet-orange seed there, an' de bush is yaller wid fruit; but dey is bitter an' sour."

"Slade, you and White go and stake off fifty acres, including those cedar trees. Molbro Janes sells his pig to buy the grave of one of his master's children, with an orange-tree growing at the head. I took him to be a sensible man, but he's a dam fool: like all Jackanapes of southern negroes he'll never learn sense. By Jove, some day when he's starving he will find that not one of his master's children would give him a morsel of food, now that they can't thrash and beat him." The three white men then roared with laughter.

In voice full of dignity, Marlborough replied, "Boss, I has been taught not ter counterdict w'ite folks, but de word you is jes spoke ain't true. You Yankee people may be dat kind, but our w'ite folks ain't. Massa's chilluns would share de las' crum' o' bread wid us, but we don't look ter dem fer food. Mars Abe Linkun is brought dem ter want; dey is neber used ter hard work, dey had all dey needed till Blue-coats come south. If you'll allow me, boss, I'll say one more word. De bes' victuals I eber eat an' de happiest days I eber lived was when I was coachman ter massa."—He bent his head respectfully in the direction of tall chimneys unsupported by walls or rafters.—"In does days we nuss an' me used ter sit under we own vine an' fig tree. Now she's sleepin' in dat cedar hedge, an' I hopes ter jine her soon."

"Hah! hah! old man, is that what you're buying?" A dead wife's grave! And the two intruders roared with merriment. "You ain't lost all sentiment if you are a free nigger, and getting old in the bargain."

"Boss, I ain't edicated: I don't know what you calls sentiment. But if it's love you's talkin' 'bout, I kin love as true as any w'ite man, if my

face is black an' my hair streaked wid grey.
Massa told us " God is love," an' he taught us ter
respect we selves, an' I hopes ter keep in mind
his teachin' till I dies."

XXIII.

News of Juno.

"To reign is worth ambition, though in hell;
Better to reign in hell than serve in heaven."
MILTON.

MIDWAY church was closed after the war. But a coloured Baptist preacher gained permission to preach in its classic-carved oaken pulpit, on condition that the cemetery be kept in order. Accordingly, at the end of his first service, he proceeded to appoint a committee to attend to this matter.

A woman arose in the congregation and spoke. It was Nannie. " Brothers an' sisterens," said she, " wid your consent I'll promise ter care fer we enclosure where massa an' missus lies. Bro' Molbro an' Amos put we captain dere too."

"Amen, amen, sister! God bless you!" responded more than one voice. At recollections of the past, many shed tears.

Nannie's care for two decades was unremitting. She kept the sweeping grey moss festooned to the limbs above, as if the spot were too sacred for touch. Feebleness and age has now interrupted her attentions.

The devotion of slaves from Green Forest is not exceptional. Many other authentic instances could be given to prove my words.

I cite but one. Not long ago, in a hotel in Massachusetts, I often met in the hall a coloured maid who reminded me of our Lydia. I greeted her with a Good-morning one day. She stopped. " Missy," she asked, " ain't you from the south ? Do you know my Miss Annie and Miss Sallie ?" She had been educated in a negro university.

" Where do they live ? " I asked.

" In Virginia, ma'am. I hear Miss Annie is getting feeble. Sometimes I think it's my duty to go and live with them. We wouldn't have anything to live on, because they are poor and weren't brought up to work. I always share my wages with them."

" How comes it you are so fond of these ladies, you must have been born after freedom."

" Yes, ma'am. It was when Mars Stonewall Jackson was tenting near our plantation. There was a big fight. Blue-coats were killing everything on the place. Missus got in a carriage to go to Miss Randolph's, across the river, when my pa came wringing his hands. Missus jumped out and said, 'Ben, drive the children to Miss Randolph's; tell her I will come in the morning if Ginnie is better.' Our white house was full of soldiers cutting up jack, and my mother has told me how old missus put on me the first clothes I ever wore. She named me Patience. Massa was brought from Gettysburg and missus planted snow-drops on his grave; but before they was blooming she was layin alongside. When my mother took her last sickness she called me one night. 'Patience,' says she, 'my appointed time is come. There is a rumbling of chariot wheels, the archangel is singing; heaven bells are a-ringing my soul engage. Promise me, Patience, when I'm gone you will always share your wages with Miss Annie and Miss Sallie. If it hadn't been for their mother you nor me would be here to-day.' Lady, do you think I could ever forget my duty to Miss Annie and Miss Sallie?"

The pathos in her voice was of itself convincing.

I give now a letter from Juno, received during my residence abroad:

Siberty Co., Ga., Aug., '94.

My Dear Missy :—

I cannot begin to tell you how glad I am to hear of you once more. Your letter reached me from Switzerland. I don't know which was greater, my surprise or joy. I am so glad to hear you are restored to health : we never thought you would be well; Miss Letha has told us of all your sorrow.

You want to know about your people. I have had ten children, seven living. Boy (Joe) is a big man and has three children and a good wife, Sissy. Matilda is also married. She is the little one, you remember, who used to beg for your balmoral, and you said " All right, I'll give it to you when it's old." I often tell the children about you. They love to hear me talk of old times. My sister Georgia died five years ago, leaving four sons and one daughter. Lawrence and Edward are still living. Mother's husband, Robin, has been married twice since mother's death. Molbro has been dead for many years. Uncle Belfast and his wife are both dead. Daniel and Phœbe are living. Many of the others have moved away or I have lost sight of them.

I have no photo of mother. But I have one of my sister, who resembles her. I will send it to you. I am glad you are writing about mother. When it is in print send me a copy, and the kind white friend who is writing this letter will read it aloud for me.

Every day I kiss your photograph you sent me; it is so precious to me! You ask if you were ever unkind to me? No, my dear missy; but you taught me many useful lessons I'm trying to teach my children.   I would love to see you once more.

We are getting on tolerably well.   Times are dreadfully hard some years.   Do write me again.

Your loving servant,

Juno.

XXIV.

Mixed Schools, Mixed Marriages.

IN Siberty County, broad areas, once teeming with cotton, corn, or rice, are now subdivided into small farms owned by negroes and northern men, who bought the land at tax-collectors' sales.

The court-house in Ashby County, where Greenville was situated, was destroyed, with its deeds and records. Seven hundred acres of pine land running back of our summer-house—also burned—were almost forgotten—the heirs were engrossed in gaining daily bread.

The judge of Ashby County convened court in temporary quarters. After calling to order, he asked, "Is there any cause why the petitioner, Samuel Thorne, junior, shall not be granted a squatter's deed to five hundred acres of pine land, on which he has lived unmolested seven years? He is an efficient officer, and has kissed the Bible over our Ironclad Oath."

A stranger arose from a rear seat, and, to the

dismay of the petitioner, replied, " May it please your honour, I protest. The said land belongs to relatives, who are not aware of Sam Thorne's kindness in squatting on their property."

Sam, Feede's alleged big black bear, years before, in a similar manner, had obtained possession of two hundred acres, where his wife Becky now lived, beating her tow-headed children as if they were made of stone.

Notwithstanding the tremendous monetary loss to us, the release from the trials connected with the care and guidance of slaves is a happy one. Our fair southland has greatly advanced with wider views of life ; the poison of internal strife is now a thing of the past. This new dawn of brotherly love reveals the silver-lining so long obscured. Phœnix-like, towns and village have risen from their ashes into cities of magnitude. Men and women walk to church, remembering their fine equipages as things of the past. Hardly a score of sensible citizens would, I believe, resume their former positions as slave-owners.

Southern women have proved their ability to prepare a dinner fit for a king. In the midst of these homely duties, year by year they spread garlands of flowers over the graves of those that —like Lee—faced the foe.

When the promise of forty acres of land and a
mule failed to materialise, the men made free were
disappointed.

Freedom to the young was a great boon; but
to the aged and sick it meant much suffering.

At a railway station in Virginia an old negro
man accosted me not long ago: " Missy, do buy
my fried chicken; it's bery tasty."

"Tell me, uncle," I said, "how do you enjoy
freedom?"

He looked me over to be sure I was northern
born, not a southerner, then said: " It's bery good,
ma'am, to know I is free. 'Fore de war I work
a leedle, eat a pow'ful lot, dance half de night,
sleep when de boss wasn't 'round. Now, I works
all day in de truck-patch. Comes eb'ry train till
midnight fer' sell dese fry. Ole Sue is sick de
bes' of de time. It takes all I makes fer pay de
doctor. De inteyor harness, what keep soul an'
body togedder, is pow'ful easy ter git upside
down. Chicken-meat what gits stale, an' bread
hard as a brickbat, don't 'gree wid we like de
sweet hog an' hominy, wid hoecake. W'en I
t'inks of ole massa's smokehouse my eyes an'
mouth runs water. Ole Sue, wid her confedera-
tion wrong, groans fer de household kitchen, or
de cabin close by."

The admixture of colour was a dreadful curse

on southern estates.   Now, one has but to note
the coppery-tinged children in large northern
cities, to realise that this evil has not abated.

The curse of this social phenomena I leave
to be overthrown by others ; merely adding,
that the Jew refuses to amalgamate with the
Gentile.   He keeps an iron band about his circle ;
who breaks it, incurs disinheritance.   Rarely do
artists put two decided colours side by side, or
clever gardeners Jacqueminots with lilies of the
valley,   They grow in the same garden, equally
prized ; but one flourishes in sunshine, the other in
a northern exposure.   The raven and dove, too,
feed in the same meadow: they never sit on the
same nest.

Then why should Julia Smith, with her flaxen
curls, occupy a school-desk with Clarence Baxter,
coloured, unless they may be free to marry ; for
intimacy often ripens into love ? Have not
statistics shown that they do stand under the
same marriage-bell ? God has made a strong
divisional line ; therefore we of the south do not
approve of mixed schools.

Why should not the negro race have every
advantage, and so make for itself a history ? They
have logical and intellectual powers, combined
with much that is good and true.   They are very
sociable, never hesitating to accost a stranger :

"Morning! is you jes from Charleston?" "Not jes at dis present minute; shortly, previous to de war I was dere, and shortly previous after de war I was dere ag'in—to-day I is journeyin' backward toward Atlanta."